By
JL Redington

©JL Redington 2017

No part of this publication may be reproduced, or stored in a retrieval system, or transmitted in any form or by any means, electronic, mechanical, photocopying, recording or otherwise without written permission of the author.

Table Of Contents

Chapter One
Chapter Two
Chapter Three
Chapter Four
Chapter Five
Chapter Six
Chapter Seven
Chapter Eight
Chapter Nine
Chapter Ten
Chapter Eleven
Chapter Twelve
Chapter Thirteen
Chapter Fourteen
Chapter Fifteen
Chapter Sixteen
Chapter Seventeen
Chapter Eighteen
Chapter Nineteen
Chapter Twenty
Chapter Twenty-One
Chapter Twenty-Two
Chapter Twenty-Three
Chapter Twenty-Four
Chapter Twenty-Five
Chapter Twenty-Six
Chapter Twenty-Seven

Chapter Twenty-Eight
Chapter Twenty-Nine
Chapter Thirty
Epilogue
Other Books by JL Redington

Chapter One

Shannon Norton was pushed back into her seat as the plane roared down the runway, picking up speed as it went. The momentary sense of weightlessness came and went quickly as the wheels left the tarmac and the plane headed skyward.

Watching the cars, roads and buildings grow smaller and smaller, Shannon wondered if she'd been followed onto the plane, at the same time wondering how she would ever know if that was the case. The plane was full, and in her estimation, *everyone* looked evil. What was happening to her? Even more important, *why* was this happening?

The drone of the plane engines reminded her that she'd not slept for several nights. As the plane rose to cruising altitude, so did her fear. Fear that she'd been followed and that she dare not sleep. However, sleep won out and she let her heavy eyelids close out the plane, the clouds below her and the drone of the great engines gradually faded from her hearing. As she slept, her mind reviewed the past thirty days, taking her back to her apartment, and to the day this whole mess began.

§§§

That morning felt just enough off that Shannon couldn't shake the nagging feeling of trouble brewing. Her grandfather had told her when she was little that she would always be forewarned of trouble. He'd said it was her spirit gift, and would guide her if she allowed it. The only thing that remained of her connection to her people in Alaska was that gift. She'd walked away from her clan, her family and her life when her younger brother, Jimmy, had called from Iowa and said he missed her. He begged her to come to Iowa; he said he needed his sister. She couldn't tell him no.

Once she'd arrived in Iowa, she found it was hard to be native in this white man's world. If she spoke of things spiritual with others around her they looked at her like she was repeating fairy tales. In the end, she began to feel like she *was*, like what she'd learned all her life was simply easy to believe because she was surrounded by people who believed the same things she did.

In the end, Shannon closed off the native part of her, and the emptiness left by that closure just wouldn't go away. Shannon felt more than ever, she needed to ground herself, find herself again, and she knew there was but one way to do that. However, going back to Alaska after having just arrived in Iowa was not possible. And without her homeland, she had no idea how to connect with the life she'd once lived, and the emptiness grew.

It was Saturday morning, and usually about this time of the day, her brother, Jimmy, jumped onto the stair landing outside her door with a resounding, thud all smiles and ready for breakfast.

Jimmy lived just down the street from Shannon's apartment complex in Smithville, Iowa. Jimmy was a wild one, with the heart of a warrior and a spirit born of courage and faith. Something had changed him, though, and when he'd called his older sister, she knew something was very wrong. Once she got to Iowa, she found Jimmy was deeply into drugs and alcohol, and the warrior had become apathetic and weak. There was anger in his heart where before there had been courage, and Shannon couldn't figure out for the life of her why he was so angry. She wanted to remind him of how his parents had loved him and how his family in Alaska missed him…how she'd missed him. She probably spoke of this more than she should have, but it didn't matter. He would hear none of it. However, the change in him was obvious, just from the look in his eyes.

The constant disagreements brought on by her desire to take him back to Alaska should have put a wedge between the two of them, but the love they had for each other was deep, spiritual. They weren't just brother and sister; they were best friends, which made it even more confusing to Shannon why her little brother wouldn't listen to her.

On this Saturday morning, so many years since she'd been back to her home,
Shannon stood at her kitchen table staring at a plate of French toast, waiting for the familiar thump of Jimmy's boots. It never came. She walked to the window of her apartment that overlooked the street to see if he was coming. There was no Jimmy in sight,

but what she did see caused fear to bubble up in her stomach and make its acidy way to her throat.

A black SUV was parked across the street and a man inside it was looking up at her apartment with a pair of binoculars. When she appeared at the window, he quickly set the binoculars down, started the car and sped away.

Shannon fought with herself all day about the car and the binoculars, certain they were looking at birds on the roof, or another apartment. But with Jimmy nowhere to be found, her suspicious nature got the best of her.

Days passed and she'd not seen Jimmy. Shannon went to work like she usually did and spotted that same SUV several times, or at least one just like it. It wasn't long before she saw two and then three; and they all seemed to keep their distance, but continued to follow her. None of them seemed particularly interested in contacting her, just watching her. When she complained to the police she was told there was nothing they could do because she'd not been hurt or threatened by anyone. Nice. It looked like she was going to have to be assaulted to get any help.

Shannon had checked at Jimmy's work early on and was told he'd just stopped coming one day and they'd had to replace him. This wasn't the Jimmy she knew. Once she'd arrived in Iowa, she'd helped Jimmy clean up and find work. He'd not missed a day of work since he'd gotten his job.

On this particular Saturday morning, four weeks into the disappearance of her brother, Shannon was upset enough that she couldn't eat. This was beginning to be a normal thing with her. Not only her eating habits, but her work had become affected, and after weeks of trying to focus she finally asked for time off. She had a month of paid leave coming and she took it. Today, determined to continue her search for Jimmy and ignore the black SUVs, Shannon grabbed her purse and coat and headed to town. She feared she'd find him relapsed into the alcohol or the drugs, possibly both, and asleep somewhere on a park bench. Secretly she hoped this would be the case. At least then she would know where he was and they'd deal with the rest together. The sleeping on park benches was how it had been when she'd first come to Smithville, but the confusing thing was that Jimmy had been clean and sober for years now. Which left her back at the same place she'd been for the last several weeks. Where was her little brother and why wasn't he at least trying to contact her?

    The downtown area was only a couple blocks south of her and she could have walked; in fact she usually did. However, today made her feel uneasy enough that she drove, just to have the safety of the car around her. Shannon checked her rearview mirror several times and watched the street, certain she was being followed. For what? Who would care about her? About her life? Their focus had to be a mistake, she was certain there was nothing of interest to be had regarding how she lived and where she went. Still, where was Jimmy and what did his disappearance have to do with her? He hadn't come for Saturday breakfast for four weeks in a row now. The fear slowly began churning her stomach again. She'd looked everywhere she could think of, reported him missing to the police, spoken with friends and coworkers. It was as if he'd been abducted by aliens. This experience almost made her a believer.

    Shannon took her usual route through the park, checking benches and watching groups of people, hoping he was there visiting with friends. He wasn't. She circled around, passing two other parks in the process, and found nothing. She called his cell phone, just like she'd done every day, and it went right to voicemail, like it always did.

There was that feeling again, the thought that something was about to happen and she needed to be on her toes. She started to turn into a parking lot and saw a dark SUV parked there, driver at the wheel. Shannon quickly stopped and put the car in reverse just as another SUV approached from behind her. She backed up as far as she could, put her car in drive, and stomped on the gas, barely missing a parked car on the side of the road. She raced out of the park with tires screaming. The SUVs did not follow her.

She couldn't believe they hadn't followed her. Was she imagining this? Had these dark SUVs always been around and she'd just not noticed them before? Her only truth at this point was the words of her grandfather. *"Your spirit gift will serve you well if you will listen to it."*

Her heart was screaming for her to head to the airport. Without another thought, she turned off onto a side street and waited to see if anyone was following her. The street remained empty, except for her. She reached into a small pocket of her purse and pulled out a well-worn business card, one given to her two years ago, by a man in her office who she'd not been able to get out of her head. But this time, she didn't just stare at the card like she usually did. This time, she would use the information on it. Admittedly, with brief embarrassment, the home address scrawled on the back of the card was in her own hand. Shannon had looked him up online and found his home address after their initial meeting. She didn't completely understand why she'd done that, but now wondered if she'd been 'instructed' to do so by the spirits. If her brain could only believe that, maybe she wouldn't feel so much like she was stalking the man.

With no black SUVs in sight, she picked up her phone and called for a taxi. When the taxi arrived moments later, she left her car parked at the curb, locked the doors and entered the taxi, calling instructions before the door was closed.

"The airport, please. Shortest route you can take."

"Yes, ma'am. Did you have luggage?"

"No. No, I, I don't. Just get me to the airport."

The driver nodded and a short time later they pulled up to the long row of airlines. Shannon pulled two twenty-dollar bills from her purse and shoved them at the driver.

"Oh, Miss, this is too much. Let me get you some-"

Shannon was out of the car and shut the door before the driver could finish his sentence. She hurried inside the terminal to the ticket counter and purchased the last available ticket on a flight to Anchorage leaving within the hour.

Checking over her shoulder every few minutes, she made her way to the gate just as the plane boarded. That was fine with her. She couldn't get on the plane soon enough.

§§§

Shannon jumped as the plane's wheels hit the runway. Her heart was racing, her eyes wide, and she swallowed several times in an attempt to calm herself. She'd slept the whole way? Realizing she was only in

Seattle, she braced herself for a two-hour layover. What was she going to do for two hours?

She found her gate and settled into a perfect spot that hid her from searching eyes, yet allowed her to see the comings and goings of her gate. She watched for passengers looking for seats on her flight, and though there were a few, they were mostly families with small children who'd missed their flights and needed other options. One was an elderly woman, escorted by her aging son. None of the candidates looked that frightening and since there were no more seats on her plane, she was fairly sure she'd not been followed. Still, the nagging doubt wouldn't leave her alone.

The thought occurred to her that maybe she'd concocted the whole thing in her mind and there *was* no one following her. If that were the case, what was she doing headed to Anchorage? Shannon immediately felt ridiculous, but realized her brother was missing, and those black SUVs *hadn't* always been there before, and the fact that they seemed to be wherever she went was definitely new. She would have noticed if this was always the case. Shannon placed her faith in the words of her grandfather and continued to watch for suspicious passengers.

The boarding call finally came and Shannon walked down the jetway with the other passengers, resisting the temptation to inspect each face. She found her seat and strapped herself in, eventually giving and attempting to nonchalantly watch the remaining passengers board. Logic told her they couldn't be on her full flight, that she'd gotten the last ticket. But someone could have given up their seat for a sad story made up by one of her pursuers. Did she even *have* pursuers?

The flight to Anchorage was several hours and Shannon felt her heart would pound right out of her chest before she ever got there. She wished sleep would come once again and she wouldn't have to think about whether help waited there or not. She couldn't help wondering if the man she was seeking would even be there. Would he even remember her? Would he be willing to help her find her brother and learn who was following her and why? It probably would have been a wise move to call ahead and let him know she was coming, but what if he'd said not to come. Refusing her might be harder in person than over the phone. She hoped so, anyway.

Flying over the snow-capped mountains she remembered her childhood. She hadn't felt her parents' arms around her for many years. There would be none of that now. Her parents were gone, and she missed them even more since Jimmy's disappearance.

Just as Shannon was beginning to think they would *never* get there, the announcement came over the intercom that they were making their final approach into Anchorage. Just getting to the gate seemed to take forever, let alone getting *off* the plane. Once she'd deplaned, she hurried to the car rental counters and quickly picked one, relieved there were rentals available. She showed them her license and eagerly signed the documents, before finally heading to the parking garage. She fought to keep herself from running to the small office in the parking area where she was escorted to her car.

It felt like hours before the lot attendant finally handed her the keys to her rental car and sent her on her way. It was late now and would soon be dark. Still, she hurried to the home of the only man she could think of who could, and hopefully would, help her find her brother.

Chapter Two

The brush moved smoothly over the mare's neck, the soft swishing sound was rhythmic and calming. The pungent smell of fresh hay filled the air and gave a heightened sense of life to the barn, the brush and the rhythm.

The horse neighed softly, obviously enjoying the gentle touch of her owner. Grant Mulvane spoke softly to her as his brush moved to her back and down her sides.

"You are the beautiful one, are you not?"

Hearing nothing, Grant stopped brushing. He stood up and moved to the mare's face, staring into the great eyes. He smiled at her, moving his arms slowly around the thick, muscular neck, allowing her to rest her head on his shoulder.

"You have no answer for me today?" he asked softly, stroking her neck and patting her. "You must forget those old memories, my friend. You have a new life, one filled with warmth and respect. The life you should have always had. Talk to me. We are friends, yes?"

The horse neighed again, a little louder than the first time, and stomped her foot.

"There, you see? We are one, you and I. We will become only closer. You know this. I know this."

Grant finished the brushing, moving back into the rhythm of each stroke. As he worked he continued his conversation with the mare.

"I have named you Noble Spirit for a reason. You have been through much pain and sorrow, and yet you have kept your strong spirit. You have overcome much, and there is more work to do. Your nobility gives you focus and direction. Listen to it; listen to your spirit. You are a strong one, gentle but firm. I respect this in you."

With the last stroke of the brush, Grant ran his hand down the smooth curvature of Spirit's back. She glistened even in the low light of the barn. The deep brown color of her coat shone in the rays of sun that snuck through the cracks in the walls and made their way to the stall.

Grant worked with her often in her stall. Remembering the terror in her eyes when he'd first found her. He wanted Spirit to know that not all men who enter her stall were bad. When Grant found her she'd been tortured with a cattle prod, causing her to unwillingly trample an unconscious man to death. When he'd first encountered her, he could tell right away the mare had been through immense trauma, and it broke his heart. When he actually determined what had happened, he was angry, and he rarely allowed himself that emotion.

He'd learned that with each prod, the mare had reared up in an unsuccessful attempt to avoid the poke from the killer. It was the killer who'd placed the unconscious man in her stall, and though she'd tried to avoid the pain of the stick, was forced up again and again with nowhere to land but on the man in her stall. This was apparently repeated until the killer was certain his prey was dead.

Being the gentle giant that she was, Spirit was broken by the experience and became tentative and fearful around humans. Somehow, when Grant approached her that day in Iowa, now more than two years ago, she'd trusted him. Because she had allowed him into her stall, he was able to find the DNA on her shoes and hooves. Once the evidence was removed, Spirit calmed down and nuzzled him, in a gesture of thanks for his kindness. It was then he knew he had to bring the horse to Alaska and help her heal. And that was just what he'd done.

It took over a year for arrangements to be made for her trip. There were health checks and shots she'd had to have to be brought to Alaska, and that took time. Then there was the issue of payment, which also took time to figure out who was to be paid for the animal, and if indeed Spirit was to be considered the property of the deceased. If that were the case, she could be part of the probate proceedings. However, traumatized as she was, Spirit was considered difficult to handle and it was in the mare's best interest for the state to accept the offer of paid transport to Alaska. It took yet more time to arrange for that transport, but finally he'd made the arrangements and she was with Grant. He'd worked with her for just under a year now to help her heal from her emotional wounds.

Noble Spirit had come a very long way in her healing process. Grant felt it was important to speak to her, important that she become familiar with the sound of his voice and with his manner. She had in fact accepted him as her new owner, but Spirit was more than a possession to Grant, and he wanted the mare to know that. She was family, just as surely as Tope, his cousin in Iowa, was family. Tope was the man he'd worked with to find the killer who had caused so much destruction, to families and to Spirit.

Grant placed the brush in his bucket and started for the stall door. Spirit followed him as if she was going for a ride.

"Again my friend?" he said, turning toward the mare. "I just got you brushed from the last ride."

Spirit pushed his shoulder gently and neighed.

"Okay, okay, but only once more and then we are finished for the day. You need your rest, and I have work to do at the house. Agreed?"

The mare pushed his shoulder again and Grant chuckled. "Okay, agreed."

He opened the gate from the stall and walked to where Spirit's tack hung. She followed him as if afraid he might change his mind and direct her back into the stall. He grabbed the saddle and flung it over her strong back. She sighed heavily, glad for the opportunity to go outside one more time.

From what Grant could determine, Spirit was very happy with her new home. She wanted to be out in the pasture or on a trail as often as he would allow it. Once she was saddled and bridled, he swung up into the saddle and pressed gently on her stomach with his boots. She responded right away and walked smoothly out of the barn.

It was a beautiful fall day, late in the afternoon. The air was crisp and fallen leaves crackled under Spirit's step, sending the aromatic scent of dead leaves into the air. Grant breathed deeply, holding in all that was familiar to him and close to his heart.

Grant directed Spirit to the familiar trail that took them around the front of the house and to the forested area beyond. They wound through the thick trees until they came to a high ridge that overlooked hundreds of acres of trees. These trees grew so close together the mountains looked like they were covered with green carpet. Spirit tossed her head, stomping her feet in anticipation of riding further. And so, on they went, until dusk was upon them and he had to hurry her back down the trail before darkness fell. It was a short ride, but a good one.

This time, brushing her down wasn't as long and as slow. "Tomorrow is another day off, my friend. We will ride again, yes? For now," he said as he dropped the brush into the bucket, "we will call it a day."

He turned and walked to the gate and this time Spirit didn't follow. She knew his tone when done was really done. She turned her head and watched him close the latch. He smiled at her, resting his arm on the gate. Neither wanted to leave the other, and she turned, walking slowly to the gate of the stall.

"You have my heart, Noble Spirit. I humbly bow to your ownership. You have me right where you want me. Sleep well, my friend, sleep well."

With that he set the bucket beside the gate and started to leave the barn, but stopped in his tracks.

Grant stood where he was and without turning, spoke as if to the air. "You hide in my barn and say nothing, yet I know you are there. What is it you want?"

The barn was still, the only movement was the swishing of Spirit's tail, but there was breathing, soft and distinct.

"I will not harm you. You may come out of your hiding place. Why have you come to me and who are you?"

Slowly, a woman slipped from the shadow into the dim light of the barn. Her waist length jet-black hair partially hid a face that Grant recognized right away. The woman raised her head and large coal dark eyes stared back at him. His words were filled with pleasant surprise.

"You! You have come a long way. Why have you traveled so far?"

The feeling at seeing Shannon Norton, the woman he'd met only briefly in Iowa, threw him off his strong emotional balance for a brief moment. He felt a stirring inside him followed quickly by a wonder of what had brought her to his barn.

"Can we go inside? I'm cold." Shannon's arms were wrapped around her body in an effort to provide some heat.

"Of course. It is this way. Follow me." Grant removed his coat and wrapped it around her shoulders.

"Thank you," she said through a brief smile and worried eyes.

Shannon followed closely in the dark, obviously unsure of the path. Grant could feel her shivering behind him.

"You come to Alaska and do not bring a coat?" He smiled softly as they stepped onto the porch.

"I...I left it in my car."

Grant opened the door and motioned for her to enter first. The warmth from inside the house flooded the doorway and she entered quickly. The scent of simmering stew filled the air, and Grant realized how hungry he was. He stepped through the doorway and closed the door behind him, removing his coat from

Shannon and hanging it on the coat rack beside the door. He strode to the fireplace, adding two pieces of cut wood to the flames, moving the wood into place with a poker. When he stood, he grabbed a throw from the back of the couch and gently placed it around Shannon's shoulders.

"Thank you," she said, wrapping the blanket further around her.

The house was a small cabin, clean and cozy. The smell of dinner cooking added to the ambiance. The entry brought visitors into a living room with low-beamed ceilings and log walls. To the right was a small dining area and a kitchen off the end of the dining room. A hallway, obviously leading to a bedroom, or bedrooms, opened off of the living room by the kitchen and dining area. The other wall, opposite the dining room was all rock fireplace. The crackle of the freshly placed wood brought the memory of her native home roaring to the front of her mind. She smiled wistfully.

Not the typical bachelor pad, Grant's home was warm and inviting, and it was obvious that much thought had gone into the arrangement of the rooms.

"Welcome to my home. Please, sit down."

Shannon saw a large overstuffed chair close to the fire and sat down, weaving and unweaving her fingers. Grant noticed her nervousness and he watched her for a moment, as she fidgeted and then buried her hands behind folded arms as if trying to find a place to put them.

He went into the kitchen and took two bowls and two mugs from his cupboard. Taking silverware from the drawer, he placed them in the bowls and grabbing the handles of the mugs with his free hand, he strode to the table. He set the table for two, not looking at Shannon but knowing full well she was sizing him up.

Grant returned to the kitchen and brought the pot of simmering stew to the table and set it on a beautifully carved square of wood. He took a ladle from the wall near the table, and scooped generous helpings of the hot, steaming mixture into each bowl. He then placed plates of bread and butter in the center of the table and poured hot coffee into each mug.

Turning to Shannon, he said, "I hope you are hungry."

Shannon rose and smiled. "That I am," she said, laying the throw over the back of the chair.

Her smile was warm and beautiful. It was the first time he'd ever seen a smile on her face and he realized he'd not even known the full extent of her beauty until that moment.

Shannon made her way to the table and Grant motioned to her place at the table. She sat down and slowly stirred the stew, saying nothing. She took a tentative bite, blowing gently to cool the mouthwatering spoonful and sipped it delicately into her mouth. Her eyes widened as she looked at her host with renewed respect.

"Does everything you cook taste this delicious?" There was no smile, only sincere surprise.

"Am I to understand the men down south do not cook?" chuckled Grant as he stirred the contents of his bowl.

"Not like this. This is wonderful."

"I am happy you like it, Shannon. But I do not think you came all the way up here to compliment me on my cooking."

He waited for her answer as he placed the small pitcher of cream and the sugar bowl where she could reach it.

Shannon pulled the spoon from her mouth and set it gently beside her bowl. She slowly chewed and swallowed, studying the contents of her bowl, as if hesitant to respond. Raising her eyes to his, she spoke softly.

"I need your help. I…I believe I'm being followed."

Her words confirmed the feeling he'd had about her, the emotion that came from her. It was all in her eyes, her rich, dark eyes, now staring intently into his.

"How long have you suspected this?"

Her response was quick and succinct. "For thirty-two days."

Grant raised his brow in curiosity.

"How is it you are so sure of the time frame?"

Shannon's eyes filled with tears and her smooth, full lips trembled. "It was the same day my brother disappeared."

Chapter Three

A single tear spilled from the corner of her eye and she quickly brushed it away. Shannon returned to the bowl of stew, afraid to look at the probing eyes of her host. Her left arm rested on the table, between their two place settings.

Grant softly placed his hand over her arm and gave it a gentle squeeze. "Please, start at the beginning. I need to know everything you remember."

Those were the words she'd hoped to hear. The touch of his hand, the warmth of his eyes, the feel of his person surrounding her…it was all she'd prayed it would be. How is it that she could've let a man like this walk into her life and right back out again?

Shannon did start at the beginning, and she moved slowly through her memory of the last month, making sure she'd left nothing out. When she finished, her face was wet with tears, tears of worry for Jimmy and at her own inability to find him.

"Did I leave too quickly? Should I have tried harder to look for him?" Her pleading eyes searched Grant's face for answers to her heartbreak.

"You have to know, Shannon, had you waited to come to me you would probably be missing as well and no one would be the wiser. In my line of work, I am usually called in as a last resort, and there is much damage done before I arrive to help. You have left a fairly fresh trail, and it may make finding Jimmy a little easier."

Grant sat back in his chair and folded his arms over his chest. "Is there anyone that you know who would want to harm your brother?"

"I…I don't know," replied Shannon, staring into her bowl and slowly stirring its contents. "He acted kind of nervous for a few weeks prior to his no show, but he was always Jimmy. He was happy and working, he had a girlfriend, or said he did. I'd never met her."

"Did this girlfriend have a name?"

"I never heard him name her, which in retrospect, seems very strange. But she worked at the same auto shop Jimmy worked at…Thrifty Auto, in Smithville."

Grant studied her face. "How about gambling? Was he into gambling?"

"Not that I know of. I know there were casinos close, but he never had any money to throw away like that."

"Did he ever try to borrow money from you?"

"No. No, he never asked me for money. He was…protective of me, and I of him. We are very close."

Grant stood and began to clear his bowl. "Can I get you more stew? There is plenty."

"No, I'm done, but it was very good."

The two worked together to clear away dinner. Grant poured each of them a fresh cup of coffee when they'd finished with the dishes. They strolled, coffee cups in hand, into the living room and settled in by the crackling fireplace. The flames lapped at the sides of the wood, still popping and snapping.

For a few minutes, Grant sat in silence, staring into the fire, deep in thought. Shannon became lost in her own thinking, neither one uncomfortable with the silence in the room,.

"Where are you staying?" Grant lifted his head as he spoke, breaking the silence.

"I don't really know. I'll get a hotel in town. Can you recommend one?"

"That I can. It is right here. Best hotel you will find in these parts."

Shannon cast a wary look at Grant and he chuckled softly.

"I have a guest room; you are welcome to it. The room has a bathroom, so there is no need to worry about shared accommodations, if you do not mind eating together. Tomorrow we will make arrangements to fly back to Iowa."

Shannon nodded and smiled sheepishly. There was no discomfort on his part, which made her feel less embarrassed and more 'at home.' She wondered if he was ever uncomfortable.

"Do you think you were followed?" Grant took a slow sip of coffee.

"I watched very carefully. I'm pretty sure I wasn't. No one followed me out here, anyway. I kept a close eye on my rearview mirror."

Grant nodded and took another sip of coffee. He watched her movements, the way she held her cup, her eyes, the corners of her mouth, her eyebrows. She'd calmed down considerably, which was good, but there was still worry etched into her face. The fear was still there as well, all of which was to be expected. The woman was telling the truth, and now he had to find a way to get to the bottom of it.

"Where did you park? I did not hear you drive up to the house."

"I…I walked in."

He knew she had her reasons for doing such a thing, and he gave her the privacy she obviously needed. "What about a suitcase. You will need clothes for tomorrow. We can walk down the drive and get that. I have no issue with you parking by my house." He smiled and laughed softly.

"I didn't bring any. I kind of left in a hurry."

"Well then, I will get you a shirt to sleep in and we will just hope you did not sweat too much on the plane." The tease in his smile was hard to miss.

"I rarely sweat," she said, smiling over the top of her cup as she took another sip. "I'll pick up a few things tomorrow if we have time."

"We will have time, after we give Spirit her daily ride and I reintroduce you to your homeland. After *that* we can shop."

Grant showed Shannon to the guest room and laid out fresh towels for the shower. He went to his room and pulled out one of his shirts and returned to find Shannon sitting on the side of the bed.

"This should help keep you warm," he said, handing her the shirt. "The nights get cold around here this time of year."

Shannon sensed there was no uneasy or awkward feeling in Grant, just kindness and compassion. Here was a man who knew who he was and was completely content with the knowledge. She envied him and he saw that in her expression.

"You will be strong again, Shannon. The strength I saw in you when I met you in Iowa does not leave. It may go into hiding once in a while, but it is always there. You will find it. Fear not."

Grant turned and left the room, turning off the hall light as he continued to his room. He shut the door and sighed. She was every bit as beautiful as he'd remembered her from that day in her office at Children's Services in Iowa. The Spirits had brought them together once again; he knew this was true. They would learn about each other as they searched for Jimmy and they would find him. Whatever happened after that would be what the Spirits wished for each of them.

As he crawled into bed and pulled the blankets over him, he closed his eyes and sleep gradually overtook him. Grant dreamed of ravens, soaring and climbing into the sky. Ravens, with eyes of coal and wings so black they shone blue in the sunlight. A Wolf watched them winging through the air, content to see them enjoy their freedom.

§§§

The lights in the house went out, though the slow burning fire gave a soft intermittent glow through the window. Lowering his binoculars, the stranger backed soundlessly into the woods, melting into the shadows. He'd found his prey.

Chapter Four

The next morning the sky shone with a brilliant blue and birds were singing in full voice. Shannon woke to the soothing sound of a tribal flute coming from the living room. The covers were warm, the bed very comfortable, and she wanted to stay right where she was, until she smelled the wonderful warmth of freshly brewed coffee wafting into her room, along with the welcomed aromas of breakfast.

She rose quickly and hurried into the bathroom to shower. Putting on yesterday's clothing, she combed through wet hair and proceeded to the dining room. Shannon found Grant in the kitchen dishing up a breakfast of pancakes, eggs and bacon, orange juice and coffee.

"How did you know I'd be ready when your breakfast was?" she teased.

"Peep holes."

Shannon gasped and Grant laughed. "I am just kidding. Please, sit, and I will bring your plate."

Shannon sat down and Grant joined her with plates in hand. He set one before her and placed one for himself before joining her at the table.

"Did you sleep well?" he asked.

"I did. Apparently when it comes to peep holes, ignorance is best."

"I am sorry, that was inappropriate. I hope I did not upset you."

"I'll contact my attorney when this is over." Shannon smirked deviously and bit into a perfectly crisp piece of bacon. "Your mom did very well teaching you how to use a kitchen. This is wonderful."

"I am a bachelor, as you can see," he said motioning to his surroundings. "If I was going to eat, I knew it would be essential that I learn to cook. I enjoy cooking, and I find great solace in my home. It is my refuge, kitchen and all." He took a bite of pancake and glanced at Shannon. "I hope you know how to ride a horse."

"I'm rather good at it, as long as someone else has the reins. Why?"

Grant chuckled. "I thought we would take a small lunch up to my favorite area and picnic. I will reacquaint you with your homeland. You are welcome to ride Spirit with me."

Shannon picked up her coffee cup and sipped slowly, once again studying him over the top of the cup. "I would like that."

"Which part?" asked Grant, with a light twinkle in his eye.

"All of it."

Grant laughed softly. "I have made the flight arrangements for the two of us. We leave tomorrow afternoon. There were no flights today, I am sorry to say. I know you are anxious to find your answers."

"Thank you for doing that."

Her concern for her brother was deep, and Grant respected her feelings. Family was important to his people and his people were also her people. Whether she remembered that or not, it was truth.

Once breakfast was cleared away, the two of them worked together on sack lunches that would fit into saddlebags. Bottled water was the drink of choice and would also fit nicely.

"You will need a jacket. I have one that will be a little big, but it will keep you warm." Grant went to hall closet and brought out a short leather jacket that zipped up the front. He helped Shannon into it and they started to the barn, lunch sacks in hand.

"You're an interesting person, Grant Mulvane," said Shannon eyeing him sideways as they walked together.

"Am I? What makes you say that?"

"Well, for one thing, I heard you talking to your horse…to Spirit, and you treat her like she understands what you say."

Grant smiled and gazed at the barn. "It is not my words that Spirit understands. It is my heart. She has no words that she can speak to me, but from the moment I saw her, I understood her heart. I speak out loud, maybe to remind myself I have a voice box, but I know if I could not speak, she would understand me. It is so with all animals."

Shannon thought for a moment, digesting what Grant said. "My grandfather used to say the same thing about animals, but I never experienced that. I envy you the relationship you have with them."

They arrived at the barn and Spirit was waiting eagerly for her morning ride.

"We are late, and she is ready to go." Grant smiled and strode to her stall. "Good morning beautiful. I have a friend for you to carry, will you agree to that?"

Spirit neighed softly and nuzzled Grant's cheek with her soft nose.

"I'm safe then?" giggled Shannon.

"Quite."

Grant led Spirit from the stall to where her tack was stored and began pulling out the items he would need for the ride. As he placed the saddle on the sawhorse, Shannon approached him.

"Oh, can I saddle her? It's been a long time and I might need a refresher course, but I would love to try."

"I will help you if you get stuck." Grant's eyes were soft and kind and Shannon could feel the sincerity of his words. She'd long forgotten the importance of conversation…true, honest conversation.

Grant watched in silence as Shannon tossed the saddle blanket onto Spirit's back, smoothing it into place. She picked up the saddle with little effort and set it firmly over the blanket. When it came time to tie off the cinch, Shannon hesitated. Grant stepped behind her and placed his arms around her, taking her hands in his. "Like this," he said, showing her the way to correctly tighten the cinch. She followed his lead and laced the wide strap through the metal rings. "Yes, now pull."

Shannon pulled firmly on the end of the cinch and stepped back, admiring her work with a wide, beautiful smile. "Wow. It's been a long time." With a slight blush she said, "Thank you for your help."

There it was. That feeling in his gut he thought he'd never get used to. If he let it, it could make him feel unsure, like walking on a narrow mountain path with a steep drop off the side. Is this what his mother had taught him about finding "that one person"? It was a feeling he would have to wear for a while to understand it better, and Grant felt himself chewing on it like it was part of the bacon they'd had for breakfast. This was going to take some getting used to, and he was certain he'd have plenty of time for that.

Once Grant was mounted on Spirit, he reached down and pulled Shannon up behind him. The horse strode through the barn and out into the warm sunshine, the soft footfalls of Spirit's hooves added a relaxing rhythm to the trail. The air around them was chilled, gently stinging their faces. He could feel Shannon's contentment.

She placed her arms around Grant's waist and snuggled into him as they rode behind his small cabin and onto a trail leading into the woods. The feel of her against him felt…satisfying. More surprising to him was how natural her presence felt in his world and how her touch seemed almost familiar.

The path wound around through thick green pines, passing open areas where the wooded mountains burst upon their view.

"I've forgotten how beautiful it is here," she whispered, laying her head on his back. She felt Grant sigh heavily.

"You have forgotten much," he replied. "But I will help you remember."

They rode in silence for a time and Shannon seemed to melt into Grant, warmed by his body.

"I need you Grant," she said, breaking the silence.

She could almost feel the smile that floated effortlessly across his face. "I do not know that I have ever had a woman say that to me before."

Shannon chuckled softly. "You know that's not what I meant."

"It is disappointing, but, yes, I do know that." He chuckled softly.

"I need to find Jimmy, Grant, and I've looked everywhere I can think of and found nothing. I need your help to find him. I can't do it on my own. He's been gone for a month now, and he never goes even a week without calling me. Something is very, very wrong. I know the men in these SUVs have something to do with his disappearance, but I'm at a loss to know what that is, and why they would be watching me."

"Clear your mind, Shannon," said Grant calmly, "and breathe deeply. Let the spirit of this land allow you to think. There is much peace in quiet places."

The scene of pine trees and well-worn trails opened to a beautiful meadow of soft grass, surrounded by trees, backed by magnificent snow-capped peaks. The sight took her breath away and she gasped at the beauty of it. Grant took her arm and lowered her from Spirit's back to the ground. Once she was down, he dismounted, taking the reins in his hand, and they walked together.

Try as she might, Shannon couldn't stop staring at the landscape. They strolled slowly around the perimeter of the meadow allowing Spirit to cool down before Grant tied her off so she could graze. Grant removed their lunch and a blanket from the saddlebags and they wandered to an area not far from where Spirit munched contentedly on the soft grass.

The air was crisp and Shannon pulled the coat tighter around her. The meadow smelled of dead leaves and pine trees, animal sweat and leather. Her senses somehow felt sharpened, more alive, suddenly aware of all that surrounded her.

They sat down together and ate a quiet lunch. It wasn't long before Grant finished eating and placed the wrapping from his sandwich in the brown bag.

"What do your parents think of you living so far away?" he asked her as he closed the lunch bag and set it beside him.

"My father died ten years ago of a brain tumor. He was a good man, a quiet and peaceful man, and he'd endured much in his life. My mother died only a few months after him, of a broken heart, I'm sure. The two of them had a love that was deeper than just words or actions. I've never met anyone who loved like they did. I always hoped I would find a love like theirs, but I'm not sure that is possible in today's world. They lived and loved in a very different time, I think."

"You will yet find this love, maybe your lives have not crossed."

Shannon studied his face, the way he moved his mouth when he spoke, the curves around either side of his lips when he smiled. "I'm not sure I believe that kind of love exists today."

"Yes, it exists. As long as there are two people who search for it, that kind of love lives. It is eternal. Always. Never-ending. It exists."

Grant's demeanor suddenly changed. It was subtle, but she felt it. He held his head higher, his shoulders back. His voice remained calm, but Shannon was aware something was off.

"Those who followed you, there are three?"

"Usually, sometimes one or two, but there was a total of three SUVs."

"Have they ever tried to harm you, or been aggressive at all?"

"Just before I left I felt like two of them tried to trap me in a parking lot, but I've had a lot of time to think about that. Now, I'm not sure the second wasn't just following me into the parking lot and I panicked and bolted. That's when I hid my car on a side street, called a cab and came here."

"You do not feel like they were trying to hurt you?"

"No, I don't. But it was just unnerving how they were always…just…there. All the time."

"I need you to hear me now. Do not move your eyes from my face. Smile, laugh, speak directly to me."

Shannon put on her best smile. "You're scaring me, Grant."

"Do not look frightened. I will let nothing hurt you. Just look at me, nod, and smile as if we are having a nice conversation."

"Well, we *were* having a nice conversation until you went all Tonto on me."

That made Grant laugh, which made Shannon laugh, at least for a moment. Grant stood and motioned to Shannon to do the same. They leisurely gathered up the remains of the picnic, folded the blanket and began to stroll slowly toward Spirit.

"There are four humans watching us."

Shannon managed a smirk and replied, "I'm so happy to hear they're not aliens."

Grant chuckled and reached out for Spirit's reins. "I only say 'human' because there is wildlife watching us as well. There is a difference, you know."

Grant stuffed the remains of lunch into the saddlebags and mounted Spirit. He reached down and grabbed Shannon's uplifted arm, pulling her onto the horse, behind him.

"You have a way of making a terrifying situation a little less terrifying." When Shannon placed her arms around his waist, he could feel her trembling.

"You started it. Tonto? Really?"

Shannon's laughter was tense, but he could feel her relaxing, at least a little.

Grant clicked his tongue and directed Spirit back to the path that brought them to the meadow. They left slowly, and not to seem spooked Grant pointed out mountains and different trails as they went, but his words were not about the landscape.

"Three of these men are together and are not threatening. But the fourth is separate from the three. He is not safe. For now, he keeps his distance, but *he* is *not* safe."

Shannon's smile froze in place. "How can you know who is safe and who isn't?"

"Dangerous intent emits a certain…scent, as does peaceful intent. One is quite different from the other. It is the same for animals."

Grant placed his arm over hers to calm the trembling. "You are safe with me. Breathe deeply and fill your lungs with this clean air. It will calm you."

Shannon felt the touch of his hand on hers. The feeling raced from her head to her toes. Her heart beat wildly in her chest, whether from Grant or from terror, she wasn't sure. She feared he would feel it through both her coat and his.

Grant removed his hand from Shannon's arm and continued guiding Spirit. "I am a tracker, Shannon. This is what I do for a living. It is a gift my grandfather identified in me when I was just a small child. My senses have always protected me, and they will protect you as well. For now, we must decide what we will do next."

Chapter Five

Grant admired Shannon's determination. The situation she found herself in was enough to make anyone run and hide, pulling the earth in over them. But Shannon wasn't doing that. She didn't talk about her fear, but he could see it in her eyes, smell it in her person. Fear had its purpose, to warn and prepare, but there were different levels of fear, different types. This fear was filled with worry and concern and could be incapacitating, but not for Shannon. It seemed to make her more determined to find her brother and learn who these men were that were following her. She was a strong one, that was for sure.

Shannon and Grant drove into town and, as promised, he gave her some time to shop for a much-needed change of clothing. Before they left for town, Grant brought her rental car up from down his driveway and parked it in front of the cabin.

While she shopped, Grant called his friends from work to let them know he would be leaving for a while. Greyson Beauchene, his boss and head Ranger at Denali National Park, was a good man, and looked very much like he should live in California and sing with the Beach Boys. Blond hair, blue eyes and a never-ending smile, Greyson was married to Aspen, a former FBI Profiler, and now mother to their son, Xander. Tony Sampezi was an assistant to Greyson, as was Grant, and also a good friend.

"Beauchene." The voice was pleasant, and the background noise included that of a young child laughing.

"How is my Godson?" inquired Grant with a grin. "His laughter is contagious."

"He's about as wild as a boy can be," laughed Greyson. "What can I do for you?"

Grant explained about his need for time off, and being the slower season, there was no problem with Greyson giving him the needed time. Grant asked that he and Tony keep an eye on Spirit for him, make sure she was fed and ridden each day, brushed and spoken to. Tony was usually the one who would take care of Spirit and Greyson told Grant he would see that Tony did his usual excellent job.

"You take care of yourself, my friend," cautioned Greyson. "This sounds mysterious, and I don't much care for mysterious. Find her brother, get some answers, and come back safely."

"I will do that," replied Grant. "Thank you."

He ended the call just as Shannon hurried toward him, a bag in each hand.

"That did not take long. I thought we would be here most of the afternoon," he said, with a twinkle in his eye. Grant took one of the bags from her and they headed to the car.

"I'm not much for window shopping," said Shannon, proudly. "I like to go into a store with a list of what I need, get those things and get out as quickly as I can. I find shopping for clothes not much different than shopping for groceries, and I dislike both of them equally."

Grant chuckled and nodded in agreement, making silent note of her shopping habits, so similar to his own.

By the time they'd gotten home from their 'picnic,' brushed Spirit and tucked her away in her stall it was well past two. The shopping had taken about two hours and Grant and Shannon returned to the cabin just before five that evening. Before she even took off her coat, Shannon went to the guest room and changed into the new clothes.

"Can I use your washing machine? I would like to have some clean clothes for tomorrow."

Grant showed her to the small, but efficient laundry room and left her to start the load while he heated up some of the left over stew. He went back to the living room and stoked the fire, placing more wood on it, then sat back and watched the flames lap hungrily at the dry wood. The smell of the warming stew slowly began filling the air.

Shannon came back into the living room and sat down in the chair across from the couch where Grant was sitting. He could feel her eyes on him and turned from staring at the flames. Already warmed from the fire, the warmth of her eyes ignited a new fire inside him, one he knew he must keep inside, but unsure exactly how he would do that. He'd never been in such a situation, and this uncharted territory somehow gave his meditations more depth than he'd ever felt before. He shook off his thoughts.

"Is there anything more you have thought of regarding the disappearance of your brother? Maybe we could talk while we eat."

"What can I tell you that has not already been said?" she asked, gazing all too comfortably at him. She rose when he did and they went together into the kitchen and sat at the already set table.

For Grant, hers was a loaded question. Maybe it was he who was beginning to feel that he had much to say that had not been said. He ignored his feelings, set them to the back of his mind, and focused on the task at hand.

"You said you'd spoken with Jimmy's co-workers. Was there *anything*...a look, a pause, anything you noticed from those conversations?"

"I went back through the visits in my mind and there was one that stood out, if only a little."

"Which one?" Grant dished up stew into each bowl as he listened to Shannon.

"It was a woman, Caucasian, blonde, very pretty. Her name was Raina and she said she didn't know Jimmy very well and couldn't help me. But there was something in the way she said it, something...I don't know. Maybe I'm grasping at straws, but I felt like she knew something she wasn't telling me."

"We will need to talk to this woman." Grant spoke more to the room than to Shannon, then sat in silence for a moment. "We should eat."

"This is even better than yesterday," smiled Shannon.

"I'm glad you like it." Her compliments made him feel...strong inside. He couldn't explain it any other way.

When they finished dinner, they cleared away the dishes, washed and dried them, and put them in the cupboard. They moved into the living room, steaming coffee cups in hand. Shannon sat comfortably in what had become her favorite easy chair and Grant rested on the couch. The enjoyed the crackling of the fire for a moment.

When he finally spoke again, he set his coffee cup on the end table and leaned toward Shannon with his elbows on his knees, his hands folded together.

"You know that I cannot guarantee we will find anything, yes?"

"I understand that," said Shannon, her hands folded in her lap. She lifted her right hand and ran her fingers gently across the top of her head and through the long black hair, bringing it forward over her shoulder as her fingers traveled down the long tresses. It gleamed softly in the firelight.

"It's just that…I've followed your career. I was interested in what you do and how you do it, and you *did* give me your card." She blushed slightly and continued. "You're good at solving mysteries, especially where people are involved. I wanted the best there is, and according to what I've read online, you're it."

"That is very kind of you to say. I will do all that I can, I want you to know that."

"I…I can't. I…don't have. I don't have a lot to pay you with, but whatever I have I'll give it to you. I have a little in savings and it's yours, no matter the outcome."

"Do not worry about payment. For now, we must concentrate on your brother. "

Tears welled up in Shannon's eyes and she blinked them back. Crying was clearly not something she did often.

"There is no shame in tears. We were given them for a reason. They clean out our souls and the pain that is there, and they comfort us when allowed to do so. You are stronger than you think you are. Your moiety…it is Raven, is it not?"

"Wow," replied Shannon with a sigh. "I haven't thought of that in a very long time. But, how did you know? It's not like I wear a sign on my forehead. How could you possibly know?"

"I dreamed of ravens last night. I am of the Eagle/Wolf moiety. My grandfather told me that is why I am a tracker. There are no trackers left in my clan, except me."

Shannon remembered how her uncle had explained the moiety to her when she was little. She remembered him saying how the clan had two separate moieties, the Raven and the Eagle/Wolf and how she must marry someone from the Eagle/Wolf moiety; that was the way of the clan and it was also a very long time ago. But now, she smiled softly to herself. *What a great memory that is.*

"You are smiling. What is it that makes you smile?"

Shannon jumped. She'd been so far into her thoughts she'd forgotten she wasn't alone.

"I was just remembering something I'd not thought of for a very long time. You reminded me of it, actually. It was the time my uncle was explaining to me about the moiety. A good memory of a good man."

"I am happy I could help. Now, where were we?"

"I was going to pay you when we get to Iowa."

"No, you are not. Let us think about how to proceed."

The quiet of the cabin was shattered by the sudden sound of gunfire. Grant dove for Shannon and pulled her to the floor, covering her with his body. The echo of the shot still in their ears, Grant held his finger to his lips, instructing her to be still. Her eyes were wide with fear, her breathing heavy.

"Stay here," he whispered. "Stay low, say nothing."

Chapter Six

Slowly and soundlessly Grant crawled to the window. It was unclear who fired a gun or what they were firing at. The house hadn't been hit, at least not that he'd heard. *Were they even firing in the direction of the house?*

Grant sat down under the window with his back against the wall. Shannon started to rise and he called quietly to her. "NO! Stay down. They could be waiting for a better shot." Peeking slowly around the edge of the window frame, he saw nothing. It was too dark outside to see across the clearing and into the woods.

When several minutes had passed, Grant motioned for Shannon to crawl to the hallway. He did the same and they met in front of the guest room door. No further shots came, no sound of intruders or stalkers outside the house. All was quiet.

Grant stood and moved slowly down the hallway toward the living room, staying against the wall. Staying in the protection offered by the windowless hall, he reached slowly for the switches at the end of the wall and turned off the lights in the dining room and living room and crept to where Shannon sat outside the guest room door.

"I will call the State Troopers. We will stay where we are until they arrive."

It was several minutes before the troopers arrived, but they could be heard coming from a mile away. Three patrol cruisers raced up the driveway and Grant stood, quickly switching on the living room lights and meeting them at the door. Shannon stayed put in the hallway, too frightened to move.

"Grant Mulvane?"

"Yes, I am Grant. Please come in."

"My name is Trace Garmon. It is a pleasure to get to meet you. You're somewhat of a legend around here, you know. Our office has not had the pleasure of working with you before."

"That is kind of you to say," said Grant, closing the door behind Officer Garmon as he entered.

Grant invited Shannon to join them in the living room, motioning for Officer Garmon to be seated. Grant and Shannon sat on the couch, Officer Garmon in the easy chair.

"Please, tell me what happened."

Grant reviewed the evening's events with the officer. When he finished, the trooper rose to begin his search with the others. "We'll have a look around and let you know if we find anything."

Grant stood as well and spoke to Garmon.

"Let me go with you. I know this area well."

Shannon's eyes widened with fear. "No, Grant, I...I don't want to be here alone."

"Shannon, there are no other doors into the house, and all the windows are closed and locked. You will be safe here. Stay in the hallway until we return. We will only be a few minutes, as the darkness will make it difficult to go very far. You are a far easier target outside than in here."

She nodded her head weakly and returned to the hallway, sitting outside the door of the guest room as she had before.

Grant stepped onto the porch with the officer, where the others were waiting. The officer began to call out orders to his team.

"Hawthorn, Larson, you two search the area to the left. Stay in voice range, all of you. Washington, Whittley, you two take the right. Grant, you, Dawson and myself will search the center area. If none of us finds anything within the first fifty feet, return to the clearing and wait for the others. Clear?"

"Yes sir."

The men headed off into their designated areas and Grant followed his assigned officers into the woods.

"There is a body in here," said Grant, with certainty. "And there is blood."

"You're sure of this?" Officer Garmon replied, his blue eyes searching more intently. Trace Garmon was tall and thin, with dark brown hair that set off the deep blue of his eyes.

"I am sure." Grant wasn't boasting, he was stating fact and the two men with him knew it.

"Found some trampled underbrush," came a call from their left.

"Cordon off the area and return to the clearing. We'll post guards tonight to keep the section secure." Officer Garmon continued sweeping the area with his flashlight.

"The body is over there," said Grant, pointing to his right. "About three yards."

The men didn't question. They proceeded to the right, Garmon keeping his light pointed to the ground, Officer Dawson cautiously searching the woods with his.

The body was face up, one shot to his chest, his vacant eyes staring into the forest canopy overhead.

Dawson pulled out some crime scene tape and began running it from bush to bush, securing the area.

"We'll need CSI out here tonight." Garmon turned to Grant. "I'm afraid it's going to be a long night for you. We'll try not to disturb you, but the lights they use will be bright and there will be conversations."

"The bedrooms are on the back of the house," began Grant, "we will be fine. Please let them know they can call me on my cell phone if they need me for anything."

"Will do. Thanks, Mr. Mulvane."

"Call me Grant."

"Thanks, Grant."

Grant hurried back to the cabin. He found Shannon right where he'd left her, huddled on the floor next to the guest room.

"Are you okay?"

Shannon's eyes were red from tears, not only tears of fear, but tears of worry and concern for her brother, tears of wondering what he'd gotten himself into, and would she ever see him again. It was all there, in the tears that made her beautiful eyes red and swollen.

"You are worried, Shannon. We have no way to know if this is connected to the disappearance of Jimmy."

"Yes we do. You can pick up the scent of that man. You know if it was one of those who were following us." Shannon's voice was sharp with certainty and frustration.

"You are right. But if anything, it should give you reason to feel comfort. This man was dangerous, the same scent from the meadow. Clearly, you are being protected, but we do not know from what, from who, or why. We will find out, but for now, you have guardians, who for some reason, are working very hard to keep you safe."

"I wish that made me feel even a little better. I'm safe, but what about Jimmy?"

"We will find that out, Shannon. For now, we should call it a day. I am certain sleep will not come easily after this, but you need to rest. We are safe now. *You* are safe." He helped her to her feet and opened the guest room door. He went into the room first, turning on the light, checking the closet, the bathroom and scanning the bedroom. He closed the blinds and stepped back into the hallway. "The room is clear. Sleep well."

Shannon walked slowly into the guest room and tentatively closed the door. Grant continued down the hall to his room and made sure it was clear, as well. He was about to remove his clothing for bed when he heard a soft knock on the door.

He opened it to find a very frightened Shannon shivering in the hallway.

"I don't want to sleep alone."

"Come in. Take my bed. I will sleep on the floor beside you."

"No. I...I don't want to *take* your bed, I want you beside me, Grant." Shannon's body trembled as she tried to explain. "I...we...Please, I just need a friend tonight, nothing more. Does that make sense?"

"I will be a perfect gentleman. I will be your friend for as long as you need me to be."

Shannon smiled sadly and moved to the far side of the bed. She turned down the covers and sighed heavily. "I'm sorry to be such a baby about this. I'm not usually like this. But…"

"You are far from Iowa," replied Grant, his voice smooth and soothing. "I understand. Remember one thing, Shannon. You are home in this land. Your roots go deep here. What has happened here tonight has nothing to do with the place of your birth. We will discover the truth, both here and in Iowa."

Shannon nodded her head, blinking back tears. Still in the shirt Grant had given her, she crawled into bed, pulling the covers over her, and closed her eyes. Grant took a heavy blanket from the shelf in his closet and walked slowly to the bed, determined to be a friend before anything else. This was what she needed right now, and he would be what she needed.

Surprisingly, Shannon fell asleep long before Grant. He lay in the darkness listening to her breathing, feeling the heat of her body beside him. More than anything, he wanted to protect her, keep her safe. Had the Spirits brought her back into his life? He would need to think on that.

Once he was sure Shannon was well into sleep, Grant rose from the bed and strode quietly to the window. Peeking through the blinds, his eyes searched the area around the backside of his home and as far into the brush as he could see. His eyes were sharp, wolf-like as he searched. He left the bedroom and went into the living room, now bright with lights from the CSI who had arrived and were working the crime scene. He scanned toward the barn, its front door visible from the cabin. Everything was secure. The brightness of the lights from the CSI search were nearly blinding in the darkness of the woods, testifying to the fact that the danger had passed. However, the wolf in him knew something was not right. What had happened that night had cost a man his life. His senses told him there was something about the victim that was…wrong.

He hurried back to the bedroom with hushed footsteps, afraid if he was gone too long Shannon would wake and find herself alone. He settled quietly onto the bed and covered himself with the blanket from his closet. The rhythm of her breathing finally allowed sleep to overtake him, and his sleep was peaceful.

§§§

It was unusual for Grant to sleep late and when he woke the next morning, his arm was resting on the waist of a beautiful woman, her intense brown eyes studied his face.

He quickly removed his arm and started to rise. Shannon pulled him back down with a softness he could not resist.

"Don't go yet. Can't we stay here for a few more minutes?"

"We fly to Iowa today, remember?"

"I know, I know. But just five more minutes can't hurt, can it?"

Grant lay back down and turned on his side to face her, his elbow on the pillow, propping his head against his hand. "You slept well then?"

"Like the baby I seemed to be last night. I apologize for that."

"No need. Life has been uncertain for you of late. I understand."

Shannon's gaze deepened, her eyes searched his. "You're not like anyone I've ever known. How are you so different? I can't even put it into words. You are…unique."

"Hmmm," teased Grant. "Unique. I am sure I have never been described as such before, not by a woman of such beauty, anyway."

"You think I'm beautiful?"

"Yes, I do." Grant paused; ready to speak again but unsure what he would say.

What was it about this woman that made his soul struggle to stay centered? It was as if everything he'd ever thought about life was still true, but was somehow shaken, or skewed. Shannon seemed to bring his world into clearer focus, yet at the same time made him feel as though gravity was failing him. How could both things be true?

"Shannon Norton, you do such things to the natural balance of my life," he said, gently moving a strand of hair from her face.

Shannon's eyes twinkled with false innocence. "I'm so glad I could help."

His discomfort rising, Grant quickly changed the subject. "I will meditate now. If I am to help you find your brother, I must find and keep my own life balance. If I do not, I will be of no use to you."

Grant waited for her to move, studying her face. She stayed put, still watching him with those large, searching, chocolate eyes. He finally spoke. "I will use your room for my morning meditation. Rest for a while. We have a big day ahead."

"No, I'm done resting." Shannon rose and tossed the covers off of her. "I'll go have a warm shower and put on a change of clothes, which is *very* nice to have. Thanks for letting me bore you with shopping yesterday."

Shannon walked around the bed as she spoke, the muscles in her long dark legs moving from calf to thigh. When she arrived at his open door, she stood in the doorway with one shoulder against the frame, her legs crossed casually at the ankles and Grant's shirt hanging to about mid-thigh.

"Enjoy your meditation." Her smile was faintly seductive as she pushed off with her shoulder, turned, and proceeded down the hall.

Grant sighed and watched her go; silently thanking the Spirits that he didn't have to think of a response. He truly didn't know if there was one in him.

Shaking his head, he sat on the floor in the corner of the bedroom reserved for his daily meditation. His legs folded in front of him, he forced his hands to relax and placed one on each knee, palm up. With a deep breath, drawn in through his mouth and released gradually through his nose, he slowly closed his eyes and began clearing his head. This was going to be difficult.

§§§

Shannon stood in the shower letting the hot water pour over her face and run down her body. She moved her hair back and let her hands fall to her sides.

She wondered silently what she'd gotten herself into. Maybe she jumped too quickly, too "spur of the moment," in coming back to Alaska. It wasn't that she didn't think Grant could help her, in fact she knew he was the only one who could.

He's so much clearer about things than I am, so confident. I feel like I'm free-falling and he's just so...there, so strong, committed, and sure of himself. I have to get a hold of myself. I have to find Jimmy and Grant is the key. Nothing else matters right now. I have to find Jimmy.

Shannon took the shampoo from the shower shelf and squirted a large portion into her hand. Replacing the bottle, she slowly massaged the liquid into her scalp and then pulled up the hair from down her back, working the shampoo in. Try as she might, she couldn't get her brain to focus on any one thing, except Grant, and he definitely wasn't a "thing."

She continued trying to untangle her thoughts as she turned her back to the water and leaned her head into the stream, letting the water pour over the long black hair.

Jimmy is out there, somewhere, and I'm here in Alaska acting like a twelve-year- old with a crush! Is he even alive? Is he hurt? I have to focus like Grant does. I have to...for Jimmy. He needs me now.

Somehow Shannon knew her brother was alive. It was as if she could *feel* him, feel his presence. What was it her father used to tell her? Something about letting her feelings guide her, or move her forward, or...*Oh, Father, I need you now. I need your wisdom and the kindness in your eyes, the constant direction of your spirit. Lead me to Jimmy, Father. Show me how to help Grant find him. Please help me keep my heart on task.*

Shannon turned off the water and stepped out of the shower, quickly grabbing a towel. She wrapped it around her and went to the sink, wiping the condensation off of the mirror with her hand and staring at the steam-enshrouded image.

"Wherever you are, Jimmy, I *will* find you."

Chapter Seven

The air outside the cabin was cold, the sky cloudy. Grant stepped onto the porch and surveyed the distance to the woods. All that was left of the events of the night before were tire tracks in the clearing and yellow crime scene tape around the entry to the forest. One police cruiser was parked in the clearing, the driver gone. Grant could hear him moving through the brush and trees, obviously monitoring any activity in the area.

Grant recognized Shannon's scent before she spoke. This morning her scent was a mixture of shampoo and body wash. It was…pleasant.

She came up behind him and spoke softly over his shoulder. "Looks like they got what they came for."

"The CSI?"

"Yes."

"They usually do." Grant sighed and stepped off the porch. The closer she was to him, the more difficult it was to think, it seemed. He turned and peered up at her. Another scent had been added to the shampoo and body wash.

"It is cold out here, Shannon. We should go inside."

Shannon nodded and turned to go back into the house. Grant stepped back onto the porch and followed her through the door.

"You are frightened this morning." Her scent was erratic, moving quickly from pleasure to sadness to peace, but the underlying scent was the strongest. The scent of fear was always there.

"I *am* frightened, Grant, but not for me, for my brother. My mind goes crazy wondering if this has *anything* at all to do with Jimmy." She motioned to the woods outside and the police cruiser, her dark eyes moist with the tears she held back. Shannon hungrily searched his face for assurance, false or otherwise. Her fear was about to take over, and Grant knew he had to help her; he needed to be her support. She had no one else, and he could feel her loneliness.

Grant instinctively placed both arms around her and pulled her to him. "We will find him, Shannon," he whispered into her ear, one hand gently stroking her hair. "I promise you. I will not stop searching until he is found."

Shannon placed her hands on his strong, well-muscled chest and rested her head there, her tears fell freely onto his shirt. He didn't care. He could feel her release into his arms, accepting the comfort.

"I know in the deepest places of my soul that you are a man of your word," she said between sobs. "I know you will *not* stop looking until there are answers. Thank you."

Grant released her and helped her to a chair. "You are welcome. When you are ready, we will eat breakfast and pack. You will need a suitcase, yes?"

Shannon smiled weakly. "You'll remember I came with very little. I'm sure I could do with a small duffle if you have one."

Grant chuckled softly. "I do have a duffle, and you are welcome to it."

Shannon stood and moved closer to the fire, placing her open palms toward the flames. Grant strode down the hall and to his bedroom, pulling out a small bag for Shannon and a suitcase for himself. He returned to the living room with bag in hand.

"Will this work?"

Shannon jumped slightly, obviously having been deep in thought.

"I am sorry to have startled you."

"No, it's not your fault. That bag will do perfectly, thank you." Shannon turned back to the fire and to her thoughts.

"There is nothing you can do from here, Shannon. We will be on our way soon."

"I know, but still, it's hard not to wonder, and harder still not to worry. Is he safe? Is he lost? Is he being held somewhere against his will? Why hasn't he contacted me? If he's safe, why hasn't he called? He's not safe. That's the only conclusion I can draw, and I can only pray he's alive."

"Pray then. There is much good in that."

Grant went back down the hall to his room and began pulling clothes out of his closet and drawers and placing them neatly in his suitcase.

He stopped as he placed a shirt into the case and turned. "Do you always watch people pack?"

Shannon smiled and walked into the bedroom. "You can tell a lot about people by how they pack a suitcase."

"I am sure that is true. What do my packing habits tell you of me?"

Shannon smiled and walked to Grant's bed, inspecting the contents of his suitcase. "Methodical, precise, kind."

"Kind? By how I pack my suitcase?" he said, laughing softly.

"No, that part of you I saw a few minutes ago. But the rest is observation from the suitcase."

"I see," he said, laying another shirt carefully on the top of the others. You have studied this process."

"I certainly have," she replied with a knowing smirk. "Your method of speech is very...old, Grant. Why is that?"

"I honor my ancestors with my words, how I say them, what I say. I owe them much, for they have given me much. Their sacrifice has allowed me a good life."

Grant finished packing and closed the suitcase, following Shannon into the living room.

Shannon moved closer to the fireplace, once again warming herself by the flames. Her one outfit was packed, along with the few toiletries she'd purchased while shopping with Grant. The bag was placed on the couch behind her.

Grant set his suitcase by her duffle and went into the kitchen. Within minutes there was hot oatmeal on the table with raisins, blueberries, milk and sugar.

"Are you ready to eat?"

Shannon hadn't been paying attention, lost, again, in her thoughts. "Oh, I didn't even help you!"

She went quickly to the table and sat down. "This looks delicious, as usual. I didn't think I was hungry."

They ate in silence, Grant allowing Shannon to be alone with her thoughts. It was difficult to watch her struggle with her emotions, but it was necessary. The wolf in him wanted to protect her, to remove every obstacle, but the eagle in him saw the wisdom in allowing the struggle. It was a hard balance for him to keep in some ways, as his emotional attachment to her continued to affect his focus and balance. *Why? Why would I allow this to happen?* Grant stared into his oatmeal as if the oats themselves held the answer.

"Is your cereal speaking to you?" Shannon giggled.

Grant smiled at her, awakened from his thoughts. "I was just thinking, pondering. Breakfast lends itself to that kind of thing. Are you feeling better?"

"I don't think I'll feel better until I'm hugging Jimmy. But until then, it's nice to have someone to be with. Thank you for being willing to help me."

Grant's phone rang and he rose, retrieving it from the lamp table in the living room. Shannon began clearing the table.

"Mulvane."

"Hello Grant, this is Officer Garmon. I just wanted to give you an update on what we'd found so far. The deceased is known to authorities only by the alias of Hammer and is a member of an organization specific to Iowa that calls itself the Brevet. We are not sure what he's doing here or what he was doing on your property. He's best known as a sniper, performing hits for the Brevet and is wanted by both the FBI and CIA, mostly for crimes against those organizations."

"That is concerning."

"Will you be available to come to the station this afternoon?"

"I am sorry, but we are leaving this afternoon."

"Where will you be going?"

Grant paused. This was going to be awkward. "Iowa."

There was silence on the other end of the line. Officer Garmon finally spoke, "You'll need to reschedule your departure, Grant. We need to hear more about why you're going to Iowa, just to rule out any connection between your trip and this sniper. When can you be down here?"

"We can leave within the half hour."

Grant went into the kitchen and began helping with the dishes. Shannon stopped, her hands wrist deep in soapy water, and looked at Grant expectantly. His face was etched with concern.

"Are you going to tell me what that conversation was about?"

"Yes, I am. That was Officer Garmon from last night; they would like to have us come down to the station. The dead man was from Iowa and we are going to Iowa. They want to know more about our trip and why we are going there. They may be a great deal of help in our search for Jimmy. I believe the more they know the better they can help us."

Shannon visibly paled. "They think there's a connection?" The panic in her was rising.

"I did not say that. They want to talk to us to determine *if* there is a connection." Grant took Shannon's wet, soapy hands in his. He turned her to face him. "There is probably a connection between these events. The more we know, the better equipped we will be when we get there. Do you understand?"

Shannon nodded her head numbly. The situation was fast becoming deeper, darker and muddier.

Chapter Eight

Grant directed Shannon into the offices of the State Troopers. Her tension level was high and she reached for Grant's hand. He could feel her trembling, and squeezed her hand reassuringly.

"You have no need to fear, Shannon. We will answer their questions and be on our way. Be strong. Tell them what they ask and all will be well. These people are not the enemy."

Shannon glanced to Grant, her hand tightening around his. "I hope you're right."

Officer Garmon led them down a long hallway to a room with a small, oblong table, with two chairs on one side and one on the opposite side. He motioned for them to sit down and Grant helped Shannon into her chair. He feared she might actually lose all use of her legs and land on the floor in a heap if he didn't get her seated quickly. Her level of fear was rising, and it appeared there was nothing he could do about it.

Garmon tossed a file onto the table and sat down opposite them. He pulled the file closer to him and opened it, laying a picture of the dead sniper before them.

"Do you know this man?"

"No, I do not, but I recognize him as the man you found in the woods outside my cabin," replied Grant. He glanced to Shannon.

Shannon eyed the picture with distaste and shook her head. "I've never seen him before."

"I'm assuming the trip to Iowa is for your benefit, Miss Norton," he said as he placed the photo back in the file. "Can you tell me why you needed Grant to go with you? That *is* why you came to Alaska, is that right? To enlist his help?"

There wasn't a flinch from Shannon. From somewhere deep inside her, Grant could feel strength and determination rising. She stared intently at the officer as she answered his question. "I have hired Grant to help me find my brother. He went missing about a month ago, and I haven't heard from him."

"That's it? You're looking for your brother? Nothing else?"

Grant turned to Shannon. "May I answer this question?" Shannon nodded, her eyes now filled with the determination he was feeling in her.

He turned back to Officer Garmon. "She has been followed since the day of Jimmy's disappearance. She does not know why and has no idea who is following her. Shannon came to me because we met two years ago when I was investigating a string of murders in her area. My cousin is a detective with the Blakely police department and we consulted with Shannon at her work, Iowa State Human Services, regarding an adoption that was key to our investigation. That is how she came to know me and why she has asked for my help."

"I see. How long do you intend to be in Iowa?"

"Until we find Jimmy." Grant replied. "I will keep in touch with you as to what we find. Especially if we find the two cases intersect at any point."

Officer Garmon relaxed somewhat and sat back in his chair. "I'm sorry to have to question you in this way, but with investigations like this, it is imperative we cover all our bases and talk with anyone that may have information."

Garmon paused and then continued. "There is an element of danger here that I want to make sure you understand. You may want help from that cousin of yours on this. The deceased was a hitman, pure and simple. We have no idea as yet who he was sent to kill, but it had to be one of you, or he wouldn't have been out at the cabin. Obviously, there was someone else there, possibly a 'would be' protector of some kind. Do you have any idea why either of you would need such protection and from whom?"

Shannon shook her head; her earlier determination appeared to shift back to helplessness. Her shoulders slumped and her chin dipped nearly to her chest. When her head came back up here eyes were filling with tears. "I don't understand any of this. I just want my brother back; he's all I have left. Our parents are both deceased and we have always been close. I want him home."

"My cousin is Sawyer Kingsley," said Grant, pulling Sawyer's business card from his wallet. "Feel free to contact him, as well as myself. I plan on seeing him as soon as I get to Iowa. Like I said, we will keep you posted." Grant handed the card to the officer. "This has his information on it, should you need it."

Officer Garmon took the card with a nod. He stood and scooped up the file and started for the door. "I see no reason to detain you, and again, I'm sorry to have to call you in like this. I hope you're successful in Iowa. Have a safe trip."

Grant and Shannon followed him to the door and into the hallway. Grant smiled and shook Garmon's hand. "Thank you. We will be in touch."

The weather was growing colder and thick clouds hung low in the sky. Grant and Shannon started across the parking lot to where they'd parked and he reached for the handle on the passenger side of the car, but stopped. Something was off, something about the car and the pavement around it. Had there been snow on the ground, he was certain he'd see suspicious footprints, but as it was, there was no way to know except by scent. The hairs on the back of his neck stood to attention and the tracker in him paused.

"Wait," he said cautiously. "I need you to go back into the building."

"What are you talking about?" Shannon stopped. "Why would I--" The look in Grant's eyes spoke volumes. She'd never seen him like this. His dark eyes were focused, not moving from the car and the ground around it. There was a sternness to his voice, as well.

"Shannon, please. You must do as I say, and you must do it right now."

"You're scaring me, Grant. What do you want me to do?"

"I want you to go back inside and get Officer Garmon. Tell him I need him at the car, and tell him to clear the parking lot."

Shannon didn't need to be told twice. She raced back to the entrance and disappeared through the door.

Grant scanned the area, buildings, trees, parked cars in and out of the parking lot, and storefronts. Was there a gun pointed at him? He felt danger, but it seemed to come from everywhere, every direction. He couldn't seem to focus the feeling into one place. This was odd, for sure.

Grant knew Shannon had delivered his message as employees and civilians raced from the building and ran to their cars. Engines started and cars began moving toward the entrance.

"What's happened?" Garmon shouted as they approached. "Are you alright?"

"So far, nothing has happened, but someone has been…" Grant paused and stared at the car. "Someone has been in close proximity of this car."

"Well, it *is* a parking lot, Grant," smiled Garmon softly, but his smile soon faded to concern. "And *you* are Grant Mulvane. I'll call in the bomb squad. Let's get back into the building. We should be safe there."

The bomb squad came quickly and searched the car thoroughly and efficiently. In a relatively short time, the squad leader had entered the station and was speaking to Garmon.

"There definitely is a bomb attached to the starter. As soon as the engine turned over the car would have exploded," he reported. "What I'd like to know is how you knew this without physically inspecting the car."

"Let me introduce you to someone," replied Garmon, turning to Grant. "This is Grant Mulvane. It was his rental car you were inspecting."

Grant extended his hand to the squad leader and smiled. "It was actually Shannon's rental car, but I was driving it this time."

The man looked stunned. "I seriously thought you were a myth. You know, the bigger than life, superman kind of thing." He continued shaking Grant's hand as he spoke. "But here you are, and I suppose you smelled the bomb or something."

Grant smiled and gently let his grip loosen, taking his hand back. "No, it is just a tracking instinct, that is all." He smiled back at the man, who was now shaking his head.

"It's an honor to help you Mr. Mulvane. A real honor." Before Grant could say anything, the man was gathering his crew and they were out the door.

Officer Garmon turned to Grant. "I'm not so sure going to Iowa is such a good idea," he said with a warning. "I suggest you stick around here for a few days and see if we can come up with anything when the device from the car is examined."

Within a second of Garmon finishing his sentence, there was an earsplitting explosion from the parking lot. Fortunately, the lot was empty of all other vehicles, as the "all clear" hadn't been issued yet. CSI had been called to come and get the car and inspect every inch of it in their garage, however, the rental, now completely engulfed in flames, exploded again as if in defiance of any further inspection. Pieces of door, seats and window fragments rained down on the pavement.

"A secondary device," said Grant calmly. "I wondered..."

Shannon had jumped at the blast and nearly landed in Grant's arms. She screeched and grabbed Grant in an attempt to become his second layer of skin.

Grant placed his arm around her and held her close to him. The three of them were out of the main office area and the shattered glass from the front windows missed them completely. Others were not so lucky.

Officer Garmon was shouting for the bomb squad, yelling instructions to others to call them back and making sure the CSI team wasn't on site yet. Others who were uninjured were calling for paramedics and tending to the wounded. The noise of terrified employees filled the room.

Grant and Shannon hurried into the open area and did what they could for the injured until the paramedics arrived.

Once the chaos had calmed a little and the EMTs were there, Garmon escorted Grant and Shannon to a waiting room away from the front of the facility and hurried back to the mess in the waiting area. Grant and Shannon sat down on the couch together. Shannon couldn't seem to hold herself together any longer. She broke into gut wrenching sobs as Grant held her close to him. His mouth said nothing, but the strength and comfort of his arms around her spoke volumes.

"What has he gotten himself into? Why is this happening? Who is doing this to us?"

Grant took a deep breath before speaking. "Shannon, whatever it is, we will find out. You are strong and capable. I can feel your strength even as you tremble in my arms. Do not give into the fear. What is important, what will help you find your way through this, is deep inside you. It will always be there, waiting for you to draw on it. Breathe deeply. You are not alone. We will do this together."

Garmon eventually returned, but it was long past the departure time of their flight. Grant was fairly sure Garmon would not allow them to go back to Grant's home as it would be too hard to protect. He was correct. Grant was explaining to Shannon that they would need to get a hotel room when Garmon walked in and heard the conversation.

"The only way that is going to happen is if your room is kept under guard. That is going to be my only requirement, but it will be non-negotiable. The only other option is that you stay here until our investigation is complete."

Grant saw the look of fear cross Shannon's face. Not fear of the situation, but fear that Grant would tell Garmon they would be staying. Fear that she would never find Jimmy. This was the fear that lay heavy on her heart, and Grant could feel that weight.

"I have made a promise," said Grant, turning back to Garmon. "I always keep my promises. We will find another flight in the morning. I only ask that you contact the rental agency and let them know what has happened. We will find a way to a hotel and to the airport."

Officer Garmon shook his head, "I kind of figured you'd say that. We'll let the rental agency know about the car. Watch your back, Grant. This situation could get sticky real fast. I'll have one of my guys take you to the hotel and I'll assign two troopers to stand watch outside your room."

"Rooms," corrected Grant. "You will need enough for two rooms."

Garmon looked from Grant to Shannon and then back to Grant. "Oh, I thought…I just… Yes, no problem. We'll cover your rooms because of the situation and we'll have two troopers outside each room. Call me if you need *anything.*" He handed Grant and Shannon each one of his cards.

Several hours passed before the two of them were given the okay to leave. It wasn't until that clearance came that Grant realized their luggage had gone up with the rental car. Arrangements were made for replacement items to be brought to them at the hotel. There had been much stress in the day, and Grant had felt Shannon's anxiety level moving up and down through much of it. Now, as they rode in the back of a patrol car to their hotel, it had reached about as high as he feared it could go. As they sat together in the backseat, Grant worked at calming Shannon. She would never be able to sleep tonight as she was.

"Take my hand, Shannon, and breathe deeply. You must calm yourself. Breathe as I breathe. Make your lungs inhale and exhale as I do." Grant breathed deeply and exhaled, Shannon watched him with large dark eyes, doing as he did.

Gradually he could feel her calming, the muscles in her face relaxed and her eyes softened. Her shoulders dropped and the grip on his hand lessened.

"You are doing well. Most people have to work much harder to do what you just did."

"I do yoga at home. It was…familiar to me…and you helped me."

Shannon didn't release Grant's hand and he could feel her pulse slowing as they arrived at the hotel. Shannon wanted adjoining rooms, and Grant understood that he would probably be sleeping on her bed again that night. But he didn't mind.

While they'd waited at the state patrol offices, Grant had rescheduled their flights and had tickets printed there. As they stepped out of the cruiser, Shannon saw the replacement tickets and quickly realized he'd booked them in first class all the way to Iowa.

"You didn't need to pay for first class, Grant. Really. This is too expensive, and you're already taking time from your work to come to Iowa and help me."

They strolled to the desk, hand in hand as Grant explained. "If I have to fly, I only fly first class." He pointed to his legs. "More leg room."

Shannon laughed softly. "You're going to spoil me."

"I certainly hope so."

§§§

Shannon blushed slightly and fiddled with her jacket. A man's words had never made her feel so…so…warm before now. Frankly, she'd never believed what men said anyway, so discomfort wasn't an issue. Why was it this man's words, just the warmth of his voice, caused her face to heat? And not just her face…she felt his touch, both physical and emotional, through her whole body. Surely she didn't believe he cared for her. Did she? What made him so different that she was willing to let the words touch her heart as they did? So much had changed in her world in the last month, and she worried about the changes to come. However, Grant was here, beside her, and her heart confirmed to her brain that she would survive whatever life threw at her.

Chapter Nine

Their rooms were very nice, large, comfortable and warm. Grant knew Shannon would not stay in a room by herself, no matter the amenities. For that reason, he'd remained dressed, waiting for her tentative knock on his door. With all that had happened over the last few days, the anxiety appeared to have stolen her strength of will, her resolve.

They'd been in their rooms for only a few minutes. Grant turned out the lights and lay on top of the covers of his bed, waiting. He couldn't help but think about the soft curvature of her face, the graceful sway she had when she walked, the way her mouth slipped so effortlessly into a smile and how easily she wore it. Her eyes were as black as night, as was her hair. But her true beauty, at least for Grant, was far more than what was obvious from the outside. Inside, her heart was strong and good. Her mind was sharp and her senses keen. Still, she had forgotten so much of where she came from and because of that, lost the knowledge of what her role was in this world. However, Grant was certain he knew, and one day, when the time was right, he would introduce her to herself…her native self, and she would be stronger than she ever thought possible.

There it was, the soft rap on his adjoining door. Grant rose and walked to the door, opening it slowly. The moonlight shone through the window of her room and lit softly on her hair. He worked hard to keep his breathing even, his thoughts on her needs, not his.

"You tremble again," he said, taking her hand and leading her into the room. "You really must stop doing that."

"I wish I could."

"*I* wish you could."

"My trembling bothers you? I really can't help it."

"It does not bother me," replied Grant, smiling at her outline in the quiet, reverent light. "It…troubles me."

Shannon followed Grant to the bed and he pulled back the covers for her.

"You knew I was coming," she said with a heavy sigh as she watched Grant. "I'm sorry I'm such a baby about this. I'm so sorry."

"I was pretty sure you would knock on my door, yes. But it has been a day of…uncertainty. And, just for the record, babies grow, but they need to be nurtured and cared for. Surely you know this. It is not a bad thing to be a baby. It is a good thing, a humbling thing. We should all be more like babies. I will help you through this, but do not worry…you will overcome your fears in ways you never dreamed of."

Shannon crawled under the covers and stared up at Grant. "Thank you for being so kind. Thank you for everything."

Grant smiled down at her. "I have not done anything yet. I am happy to help you."

Shannon reached up and took his hand. "You have done more already than you know."

Grant squeezed her hand and reluctantly let it go. He found a spare blanket on the shelf in the hallway closet, pulled it down, and made his way back to the bed. He lay down beside Shannon, spreading the thin blanket over him. It would be a long night feeling the warmth of her so close to him.

"You're going to be cold, you know," said Shannon, turning onto her side and facing him. The moonlight now stroked the softness of her skin and sparkled in the darkness of her eyes.

Grant turned onto his back, studying every inch of the ceiling, to avoid actually *looking* at her. His heart beat wildly inside him, as it had only one other time in his life. His mind wandered back to a different darkness, when he was a young boy and was hunting with his grandfather.

It was early morning in the forests of the village and Grandfather walked silently over the branches and needles. Grant understood that he was to do as his grandfather did. Grandfather was an excellent example.

A scent wafted up from the ground before Grant and hit his senses hard. It was strong enough to make his eyes water, and he touched his grandfather's arm.

"Grandfather," he said softly, "do not step again. There is a track before you and I must see it." His grandfather stopped and shined his flashlight on the ground. There, before him, was a large track. He smiled at his grandson and stepped back, patiently.

Grant moved forward and knelt beside the track. "It is an elk, and he is injured."

"How is it you know this, young one?"

"I...I do not know. I...I think I can smell it, and...and...my heart beats in time with the elk. He is not far from us, Grandfather, and he is frightened and cannot help himself. He is young, like me. His heart beats at a rapid pace. He is hurting."

"We will find the elk and help him. Then we will talk."

They found the elk that night, caught in the trap of a white poacher. Grant moved to the head of the animal, close to the growing antlers and sat down, unafraid of the danger. The animal's eyes were wild with fear. Grant touched the elk's soft nose and spoke to him in hushed whispers.

"Do not fear, my friend. You are safe with us. My grandfather will fix your leg if you will allow it. Will you...will you allow it?"

The huge animal stopped struggling, his breathing ragged and hard. "Our hearts beat together, yes? I feel it...you feel it. Be still now. Be very still."

Grant watched the nimble hands of his grandfather as he worked quickly, to free the elk from the trap. As he removed the metal from the elk's leg, a low moan escaped from the exhausted animal. He was in much pain.

Next, Grant watched his grandfather remove the vest he wore under his large coat, then replace the coat. He took a small pouch from his coat pocket and opened it carefully. Grant had seen this pouch of salve many times and had felt its soothing warmth on many childhood wounds.

Grant spoke softly and soothingly to his friend as he watched his grandfather carefully spread the ointment over the wounds on the leg. The native child watched as his grandfather cut the long vest into wide strips, wrapping the strips around the wounded leg and tying them off tightly.

"You are doing very well," cooed Grant. "You will heal now and be strong again one day. I am sorry about this trap. This one will no longer hurt you. You must watch for these."

The elk studied Grant, and the boy could feel the probing. "Yes," he said, "we are brothers now. I will never forget you."

"Well?" The voice came out of nowhere and suddenly he was back in the hotel room with a beautiful woman lying beside him.

"What do you ask me?" Grant had forgotten the conversation he'd left for the forests of Alaska.

"I *said*," began Shannon, "that you're going to be cold in that thin blanket. Where did you go?"

"It is late, we should sleep. We have a big day ahead of us."

Shannon rose up on one elbow. "That's it? We're going to sleep now? I like to talk before I sleep."

"You live alone. You must talk to yourself before you sleep," chuckled Grant. He turned his head and gazed at her. "You no longer tremble. I am interested. Do you tremble on demand?"

Shannon slapped his stomach playfully. "Very funny. I'm not scared when I'm with you." She lay down on her back and stared at the rays of moonlight making their way across the room. "I want this over, Grant. I'm not accustomed to feeling so unsure, so at war with my own thoughts."

"I understand," replied Grant.

"How can you understand? You've never been insecure a day in your life."

Grant rolled onto his side and faced his bed partner. A kindly smile brushed his lips. "Oh, but I have, Shannon. Now, go to sleep."

Shannon turned her head toward Grant, her eyes moist with unshed tears. "I'm sorry to put you through this. I'm sorry to have asked you to help me find my brother."

"Have I complained? We will find him. Now, go to sleep."

They lay in silence for several minutes. Finally Shannon's sleepy voice whispered through the darkness, "I'm going to make you tell me about that time… Grant…that time when you…felt…insecure." Her words became murmurs as she drifted off to sleep. "I really am."

Then I will have to tell you it is you *who makes me feel that way.*

Chapter Ten

The next morning was cold, but the skies were clear. Shannon and Grant readied themselves for the day and proceeded to the restaurant downstairs for some breakfast. Grant dismissed the guards who'd been standing outside their rooms. They protested, explaining they were under orders. However, Grant was insistent that they could handle the day on their own. As the men left they were calling the office. He expected to get some flack for that from Officer Garmon.

"Well, okay, then." Shannon was teasing him. "I'll eat downstairs, but it's not going to be the delicious breakfasts I've become accustomed to."

Grant laughed as they stepped onto the elevator. "You will have to settle for store bought cooking, I'm afraid. I didn't bring my cookware, and I never cook without my cookware."

"Really?" Shannon stared at him in surprise.

"No. Not really," he teased.

"You know, I never know when to believe you or not. You're impossible."

"You sound like my mother."

The comment brought a good laugh from Shannon. "I would like to get to know your mother. She seems like my kind of lady."

The elevator doors opened to the main lobby and they made their way to the restaurant on the same floor.

They were led to a booth and each sat opposite the other. The waitress handed them a large menu and they began searching through the items listed.

Returning after a few minutes, the waitress quickly took their orders. Once she'd left they sat in silence for a bit, both lost in thought.

"Penny…" Shannon was smiling at him from across the table, her chin resting in her hand. Long fingers curved up the side of her face.

"What?" he said, having been pulled back to the present. "What do you mean…penny?"

"For your thoughts," she giggled. "A penny for your thoughts…surely you've heard that. My mother used to say that to my dad when he'd crawl inside his own head and become lost in thought."

"Ah, yes, I have heard that. However," Grant's eyes sparkled mischievously. "it will cost you far more than a penny to hear my thoughts. I am pretty expensive."

The waitress interrupted the exchange as she placed the steaming hot plates before them.

"What time is our flight today? I keep forgetting to ask you." Shannon picked up her coffee cup and blew gently on the hot contents.

"It is five o'clock. I was not sure what this day would bring, so I made it later."

"After yesterday, I think that was a wise decision." Shannon smiled at him over her cup. "You have spoiled me. This coffee is awful." She set the cup back on the saucer and concentrated on the food before her.

"When are you going to tell me about you, Mr. Mulvane? I know very little about your life. Do you have brothers? Sisters? Are your parents still living?"

"My parents have gone on, I had one brother who died of a drug overdose, and a sister who died when she was small."

Shannon stopped and stared at him. "You're alone then."

"I am never alone. I carry my family with me, here," he said, laying his hand over his chest. "They are always with me, guiding me and helping me."

Shannon was quiet and continued eating. After a few minutes had passed, Grant spoke. "You do not think this is so?"

Shannon played with her food for a minute before laying her fork down and staring across the table at Grant. "I...I used to, I guess. It all seemed so real when I was young."

"It is real."

"I know, I know. But when I moved to Iowa to be with Jimmy, everyone kind of acted like that was a silly belief system. Like it was bogus tradition. I mean, at first I paid no attention, but soon it became uncomfortable. I was in school and finishing up my degree in Social Work. My classes included a section on the belief systems of different cultures, but somehow I felt like when they spoke of these things, they were presented as...I don't know...nice thoughts."

Grant thought for a moment. "Shannon, when someone who is not of a culture and they try to teach the traditions and customs of those cultures, there is no spirit there. There is no guide to teach the truth of those traditions. Without the spirit to guide you, they would seem, as you said, nice thoughts."

Shannon leaned back against the seat and Grant continued. "It would be like a parent sending their child to boarding school and then believing that the family traditions and customs would be taught to that child. It will not happen. It is a parent's job to teach those things, to live them. I know you were an adult when you left the clan, but it is more difficult to practice your lifestyle when you are doing that alone. What does Jimmy think of our culture?"

"Jimmy lost his faith long ago. He abandoned our beliefs long before he left the clan. My parents were afraid for him. I was afraid for him, and now look at me. I did exactly what he did. I just learned to live a different way. So did he. We're not bad people, we just live a different life than that of our family."

"You cannot walk away from your family and not feel a loss," replied Grant. "It's not a matter of good or bad, it is a matter of family, of having a life you believe in, something above the every day. But, you must find this out on your own. One day you will remember your family, your life."

They stood to go. Grant turned once more to Shannon. "You will need your clan, your mother, your father, even Jimmy, to help you find Jimmy. If you can find them inside you, you will be whole again. Life will not frighten you, but you will be renewed every day. And they will help you in your search, for your brother, and for your life."

Grant paid the tab and they walked through the double doors to find a State Patrol cruiser waiting for them. Trace Garmon stood outside the driver's side of the car, and stared over the cruiser at them.

"I didn't think we'd seen the last of you," joked Grant.

Officer Garmon chuckled. "I was warned about you. I was told that you liked to do things your way and I can appreciate that. So do I. Get in the car."

Shannon raised her eyebrows and smirked at Grant. "Sounds like they're on to you." She slid into the backseat and Grant climbed in beside her.

"Don't believe everything you hear," he said.

They pulled out of the parking lot as Officer Garmon updated them on the progress of the bombing investigation.

"I'd planned on coming down here anyway," he laughed, "but I should throw you both in jail for dismissing my detectives."

Shannon turned a shocked face to Grant. "He can do that?"

Grant couldn't help the chuckle that escaped his lips. "No, he cannot. I think he is telling me that he is the leader of his pack, not I."

"Correct," laughed Garmon. "Now, about that investigation. There wasn't much left of the car, so getting any information from that second bomb was a no-go. However, we were able to retrieve information from the first bomb, due to your quick thinking, Grant. Unfortunately, it contained all common wiring. We're in the process of speaking with suppliers in the area to see if they remember who purchased the wiring, but we're not hopeful. These guys usually cover their tracks pretty well. So, I guess the update is that we've turned the information over to the FBI. Since you were having issues before you got here, Shannon, and those issues continued once you got here, we could get the FBI involved as there was a crossing of state lines by the perp or perps."

They pulled into the airport and up to the entrance to the terminal and Officer Garmon turned to the backseat. "Thank you for all your help. We will be in touch."

Shannon and Grant exited the car. They had basically the clothing they were wearing, which is how Shannon had arrived in Alaska anyway. Grant would pick up a few things once they got to Iowa.

Once through the TSA checkpoint, they continued on to their gate. They wouldn't board for several hours and so they found seats in the waiting area. Grant stared out the window at the beauty that was his home.

"What are you thinking about when you look out there?" Shannon leaned forward to see Grant's face.

"I am thinking about you and Jimmy."

"What about us?"

"Jimmy is sacred to you."

"Yes. Yes, he is. Though I've never thought of it that way, but it's a perfect description of how I feel about him. How I've always felt about him."

"What else is sacred to you?"

"I don't know what you mean." Shannon's eyes studied him, her brows knit, her face intent.

"I mean, what is sacred to you in addition to Jimmy?"

"Nothing. Jimmy is everything that I hold sacred. He is my brother, and he's all I have. There is nothing more important to me than he is."

"What about you?"

"Me?" Shannon whispered. Then, recovering she asked, "Why would I be sacred to myself?"

"Shannon, look outside that window. Do you see the trees, the mountains?"

Shannon nodded.

"The ground they grow out of is sacred ground, therefore, the trees and the mountains are sacred. If this is so of a landscape, of dirt and rock, how could it not be so for you as well? If you ignore your own worth, you squander something that is holy. Remember this. Remember this always. *You* are sacred. Your ancestors are counting on you to live your life in such a way that you honor not just the family you were born into, *which includes you*, but your future family as well, which includes your unborn children and their father."

Grant sat back and let his words sink in. Shannon was quiet.

"Come," said Grant standing and holding out his hand to her, "we will walk for a while."

They wandered the airport for several minutes. While Shannon browsed a few gift shops, Grant waited in the walkway, standing beside the windows and staring out at the world around the airport.

"You love Alaska, don't you," she said, coming up behind him and setting her chin on his shoulder.

"Yes, I do. However, it is true that I love all the land, the earth as a whole and all who possess it. There is evil here, I do not love that. But all that is not evil, that is what I love."

"I don't understand how you can say you love someone you don't even know, places you've never been."

"I can do this because there is only one earth, but amazing in it's variety of dirt, rock, vegetation, animal and people. The Great Creator made all of this. The variety you see here is to be cherished not hated. Known or unknown, we are all one with the earth and sky. This beauty, this abundance is ours, equally, put here to be cherished."

They walked for a while longer and finally began to make their way back to their boarding gate. Shannon was quiet for most of it. As they sat down in the waiting area, she turned to Grant.

"What you say is so beautiful. Can it really be true?"

"It can and it is true. I speak what is in my heart, and the heart is always true."

The call came to board and within a few minutes they were seated comfortably in first class seats.

"I've never flown first class before," said Shannon, her eyes taking in every inch of her surroundings.

"I never fly any other way. It is hard for me to think when I am in a cramped space."

"That's for sure," agreed Shannon. "I can hardly breath in coach. I feel like flying is an encroachment on my personal space. I rarely fly for that reason."

The plane began the take off, taxiing to the end of the runway. Once cleared, Grant and Shannon felt the familiar pressure of gravity and the plane sped faster and faster down the runway. Within seconds, the wheels left the ground and they were on their way.

Shannon was soon asleep. Grant knew she needed the rest. The tension of the past month had taken its toll, and he was grateful she could sleep. Gradually her head fell gently on his shoulder and he didn't try to adjust it. The feeling of her leaning against him was warm and personal. She fit him, and he fit her. Gradually Grant's eyes closed and he was back in his village speaking with his beloved grandfather.

Chapter Eleven

"Grandson, tell me more about how you knew of the young elk."

The fire burned softly in the fireplace of his grandfather's home. Outside there was a large teepee that stood in back of the home and was used for special ceremonies. Today, they were inside the log home, warming themselves after their morning in the forest.

"I do not know how to explain it."
"Try."
A sigh welled up in the young boy and exited heavily through his mouth. "It was sudden, Grandfather, I was not expecting it. I felt the scent when it hit my nose. I didn't smell it, I felt it. It felt like danger, pain and sadness. When I knelt at the hoof print, I knew that it was the scent of an elk, and I knew he was young and in trouble. I...I just knew these things, my Grandfather, I...I do not know how I knew them, but I did, and it was so strong I wanted to run and find the animal, but I stayed with you."
"Son of my son, I have prayed that the Spirits would send a tracker, a watchman to our family. One

who can see what no one else can see, who can feel what others do not feel. It is you, my grandson; this is you, and you are destined for greatness."

"I do not desire greatness, Grandfather."

"And that is why you shall be great."

Several months passed, Winter came and its departure brought spring. Grant walked alone in the woods, enjoying the feel of the ground beneath his feet and the cool air surrounding his body. He wrapped himself in the stillness of the early morning. Fog lay like a whisper on the ground.

This was not the same forest he'd visited with his grandfather, but he knew the place well. This was one of his favorite spots to meditate when he needed to be alone. He gazed around him and his eyes came to rest on the figure of a magnificent animal, an elk, strong and tall. It was his friend. Recognition was instantaneous in both boy and beast and they moved slowly toward each other. The great elk lowered his head and allowed forehead to gently rest against forehead. There was no fear in either of them. Grant sensed not just the friendship, but also the strength and power of the great beast. He sensed something else as well, an offering from his friend, a gift of that strength and that power. Grant felt the gift enter him and settle comfortably in a place deep inside him, becoming part of him.

The experience was one of great meaning for Grant, and one of many times the two friends would meet. Always in that same place, always as friends, always as souls stitched together in a time of need.

One day his friend did not come, and the boy never saw him again, but the elk's memory remained, forever united with his spirit like a warm blanket, and the gift given him by the great elk would forever be with him.

Grant woke to the whine of the landing gear as it lowered and 'thunked' into place for their gentle touch down in Smithville. He gently moved Shannon's arm, and she stirred slowly, a satisfied smile gliding gently across her lips.

It took a few minutes to force her from what Grant thought must have been a great dream, but she finally sat up and stretched. The plane rolled to the loading bridge and stopped. The air filled with the click of multiple seatbelts unfastening.

They disembarked and, as they had no luggage, went straight to the car rental agency. Grant rented a car and they proceeded downtown to find Shannon's car right where she left it. Rather than risk another incident, Grant called the police department and explained that he would like the SUV checked for a bomb, possibly two, and why. The police and bomb squad arrived in a very few minutes and after thoroughly checking the car, found nothing. Grant thanked them and once they'd assured the squad leader they were in good hands, namely those of Sawyer Kingsley, the squad returned to the station. The men were quite familiar with Sawyer.

"Let's go drop the rental off at the airport and we can use my car, if you're good with that." Shannon was searching for the hidden key container in her car's engine compartment. Once found, she unlocked the door and Grant followed her back to the airport.

They returned the rental and Grant joined Shannon in her SUV. She was ready to jump into the fray.

"Where do you need to go first, Grant? What do you need to do?"

"First ,we need to find a hotel, as we are both exhausted and that will not serve us well tomorrow. As I recall Blakely is about three hours from Smithville. Is that correct?"

"It *was* three hours but the state built a freeway between Blakely and Smithville and cut the time to just under an hour. How's that for efficiency?"

"I like it," replied Grant with a twinkle in his eye. "I will call Sawyer and make sure he has time to adjust to my coming. He owes me one."

"I just want to find Jimmy, and being back in Iowa only makes it harder to not be out there looking every minute. I would rather get to work."

Grant studied Shannon's profile before speaking. "Shannon, this is going to be a process. You understand that, right?"

"Yes, but I've already done most of the work, talking to his employer and searching for him everywhere I could think of, checking the hospitals…" Her voice trailed off.

"That was good thinking, but there are also employees to interview. Did you search his apartment?"

"Well, actually, no, I…I don't have a key to his apartment. Okay, I did, but I lost it. It was hanging on a cabinet hook in my kitchen and I must have taken it down. It's probably in one of my purses."

"Do you know that for a fact?"

"No."

"This is important, Shannon. Do you remember removing it? Did you go to his apartment for any reason?"

"He always came to my house. I wanted to search his apartment before I left, but I couldn't find the key and since I wasn't listed on the contract, the landlady wouldn't let me in."

"Did you happen to ask her if she had seen anyone else entering or leaving his apartment?"

"What are you saying, Grant? That someone stole my key and used it to get into Jimmy's apartment? That's ridiculous. If they wanted in they'd pick the lock or something, wouldn't they?"

"I am only checking details, Shannon. Jimmy may have taken the key himself when he was at your house for breakfast. He may have needed to give it to someone for whatever purpose. There is no way to tell why it is missing, but it is concerning that you do not remember when it disappeared or how."

"He would have told me he was taking it." Shannon didn't sound convincing.

"He may not have wanted you to know. I'm sure these things will all come together as we go along. You said he always came to your house for breakfast. Did he ever say why?"

"No… But I always thought he was uncomfortable because he maybe didn't have any furniture or because his apartment wasn't very nice. I don't know. He was just very clear that he wanted to meet at my apartment."

Shannon's eyebrows knit and she began chewing her lip. Her hands gripped the steering wheel and slid forward and back over the smooth surface, obviously not even realizing she was doing it.

"You need not be concerned about these things, Shannon. They are only small details to add to the known information."

She turned her head, glancing quickly into the darkness outside and returned to the road ahead. When she did, her eyes were filled with tears and they quickly began spilling down her cheeks. One hand flew to her mouth in an effort to hide the sob that she couldn't keep inside.

"Pull over, Shannon."

"No…no, I'm fine." She could barely choke out the words.

"Shannon, pull the car over." Grant's voice was firm, but the compassion he felt for her was strong.

She slowed the vehicle and proceeded to the side of the road. The car stopped and Shannon placed it in park. Dropping her head hopelessly on her hands, still tightly clinging to the steering wheel, the sobs poured from her as if they came from her very soul.

Grant unfastened his seatbelt, got out of the car and went around to the driver's side. He opened the door. "Come here," he whispered softly, taking her arm and pulling her to him. She came willingly, slipping from the seat and falling into his embrace. Her head fell onto his chest. "Shannon, this may get harder before it gets better, but I want you to know that I am here for you. I will be your guide through this, if you will have me."

"Why didn't I think of these questions? They're so obvious! Maybe I could have found him sooner. What else didn't I think of? What else have I overlooked?"

The sobs came harder now, her disappointment in herself for not looking deeper, the grief for the loss of her brother, both causing her broken heart to break even more.

Grant held her close to him, saddened by her pain, knowing she had much more strength in her than she felt at this moment.

"You did everything you knew how to do. You are not an investigator; you cannot be expected to think like an investigator. You did everything you could think of, and once you could not think of anything else, you came to me. That was the right thing to do. We will work together, and when you need to cry, I will hold you. Until you discover your own true strength, lean on mine. I will always have enough for both of us."

Chapter Twelve

Shannon and Grant sat in the SUV on the side of the road for several hours talking. She needed the time, needed to know there was someone she could count on to get her through the ordeal of finding Jimmy.

It was the early hours of the morning when they parked Shannon's car in the lot of a nice hotel. Grant had taken over the driving, as it had been an emotional evening and the effect on Shannon was obvious. Grant was thankful Shannon had slept as much as she had on the plane. She would need more now. She looked exhausted.

Rather than take her home and then go check into a hotel he decided to just head to a hotel. He knew she would argue with him about staying at her place, and he didn't want to put her through all of that. However, it appeared they would have the conversation anyway, but at least they would already be on the way to the hotel.

"Why are you parking here? I have an apartment here, you know."

"We're staying in a hotel tonight."

"But my apartment is five minutes from here!"

"I know, Shannon, but let me ask you…is the bed in your guest room already made?"

Shannon's shoulder's slumped. "No."

"I thought not, and you are far too tired to deal with it. We will stay here and go to your apartment in the morning. You will rest better here tonight, without worrying about whether or not I am comfortable and all my needs are being met. You do not need that pressure tonight. You need to rest." He got no further argument from Shannon.

They checked in at the desk and went right to their rooms. This time there was no knock on the adjoining door. Grant knew Shannon needed some time to clear her head and he hoped she would sleep. Still, he found himself missing her presence beside him.

He'd stood at the adjoining door several times, hearing her weeping softly into her pillow. He nearly knocked on the door, but his heart told him not to, and he understood why. Shannon would clean out her pain with those tears, and she needed to do that. However, it was difficult for him to allow her to do that on her own.

When he could no longer hear her crying, Grant stopped checking the door. He stayed in his bed and tried to turn off his senses. It didn't work well, and though he wanted to go to her, he struggled to do as the Spirits directed him and give her the space she needed. Sometime in the night Grant finally slept.

He woke early the next morning and spent some time in meditation. As he closed his session, he stood and at the same time heard a soft rap on his door.

He opened the door to a Shannon, who stood before him with swollen, red eyes and a sad smile.

"You are better?" Grant reached out to her and she fell into his arms.

"I am better," she whispered. "I've never had anything in my life consume me like this has. I can't help but wonder if I've lost my sense of self in all of this. It's as if I've fallen into a hole and can't figure out which way is up."

She stepped back and sighed. "You slept well, I hope."

"I did," replied Grant. "I was concerned for you, but the Spirits said you needed to be alone. It probably feels like your tears have turned the land around you to mud. It happens sometimes when we struggle with emotions. Come, sit down. We will talk for a moment."

He led Shannon to one of two chairs set beside a small table. She sat down and he moved the second chair so their knees nearly touched. He took both of her hands in his.

"You must never lose sight of who you are. You have Spirits that guide you, Shannon, but you are trying to handle all these emotions by yourself. We were not created to do this. We need our guides to show us the way. They not only guide us; they heal us and keep our mind focused with their wisdom. I will show you how to hear the Spirits. You have only forgotten how to listen for them. They have never left you."

"I...I can't... I'm not sure I still believe in those things anymore."

"It is up to you, Shannon. I do not wish you to feel uncomfortable, however, I do want you to know you have help if you want it. I am always here."

After a quick breakfast, Grant and Shannon headed to Blakely. Grant put in a call to Sawyer while they were on the road.

"Kingsley."

"It is good to hear your voice, Cousin."

"Grant? Is that you?"

"Yes, it is. Are you at work or are you being lazy and playing with that little one?"

"Lazy…" he scoffed at the word. "I wish I was being lazy, but no I'm at work. Where are you?" Sawyer's question carried a hint of suspicion.

"I'm on my way to your house, about forty-five minutes away."

"You're *what*?"

"If you are at work, though, we will just go to your office and meet up with you at the station. Are you okay with that? I am going to need your help, and it will be out of your jurisdiction, and may require special permissions. What do you think?"

"I think you better tell me all about it when you get here. I'll speak with the captain and prep him for your arrival."

They ended the conversation and Shannon was smiling. "I remember Sawyer. He was funny…I mean, he kept looking at you toward the end of our meeting that day in my office like you were forgetting something. He just seemed…funny."

"He thinks himself much funnier than he is, but he certainly makes me laugh. You look like you are feeling better."

"I am. I appreciate you letting me cry it out last night. It really did help. By the end of it, I was so tired I couldn't hold my eyes open, and at that point I knew I'd gotten it all out."

"I am sorry if I said something that made the tears begin."

"No, it wasn't you, Grant. It was all me. The conversation just prompted all of my fears, frustrations and anxieties to come to a head, and I just lost it. But, in retrospect, I think I needed to do that. It…it cleaned out my heart and now I feel that I can think clearly. A great weight has been lifted from me. I know having you with me is part of that."

"I am happy to be here."

Shannon reached over and squeezed his hand. "Thank you."

They arrived minutes later in Blakely and went straight to the police station. Blakely was a small, quiet town with an equally small police force. Sawyer's main duties were as a detective for the department, and he was very good at his job.

Entering the station they proceeded up the stairs and into the bullpen. Straight ahead, through the maze of desks and desk chairs was Captain Chase Amerson. A straight, to the point man, Captain Amerson was easy to get along with because everyone always knew where they stood with him. Grant liked him. Also through the bullpen but to the right of the captain's office, was Sawyer's office where Grant and Sawyer spent many hours sifting through tips and evidence on the case they worked together.

Shannon followed Grant to Sawyer's office. She recognized Sawyer right away and smiled at the reunion of the two cousins. Sawyer stood a little taller than Grant, and there was no resemblance. Sawyer's deep green eyes were large with dark lashes. His hair was a light brown, where Grant had dark brown eyes and long black hair held together by a leather strap tied at the nape of his neck.

"Grant! It's good to see you again." He stood and gave Grant a large bear hug before realizing Grant had brought a friend. Stepping back from Grant he stuck out his hand to Shannon. "I remember you. You're…uh…"

"Shannon," she said shaking his hand. "Shannon Norton. We met at my office in Smithville. Department of Children and Family Services."

"Yes, that's right," smiled Sawyer. Grant could tell Sawyer was working very hard at not smirking. It was almost comical. "Well, come in. Sit. Sit. Tell me what's going on and I'll see if I can help."

Shannon was just about to start when Sawyer's partner came through the door. "Hey Sawyer I-"

Tope Daniels looked up from the documents he was reviewing and realized he'd interrupted the meeting. "Oh, I'm sorry. I can come back later." He started to retreat and Sawyer stopped him.

"Tope, wait. You're going to need to hear this, I think. Come in, have a seat. Grant, Shannon, this is my partner Tope. He'll be working with us. Captain Amerson has given me the go ahead to help with whatever you need. Have a seat, Tope."

Tope shook hands with Grant and Shannon and pulled a chair in from the bullpen. He stood just under six feet tall with dark hair and clear blue eyes. He was confident and sure, and Grant knew immediately he was a man of great integrity, a good match for his cousin, Sawyer.

"Shannon was just about to fill us in on what's happening," he nodded to Shannon. "Go ahead, please."

Shannon related her experiences prior to her trip to Alaska. When she finished, she turned the rest of the story to Grant.

Grant explained about the feeling of being watched, the shooting at the cabin, the explosion at the office of the Alaska State Patrol and their arrival in Blakely.

Sawyer glanced at Tope. "What do you think?"

Tope sat forward in his chair. "I think we need to check out Jimmy's apartment and then his former employer."

"Agreed," said Sawyer. "How about you two, does this work for you?"

"That is exactly what I have been thinking about," said Grant, thoughtfully. He paused for a moment before speaking again. "There is much to this case that sleeps beneath the surface of what we have seen so far. I believe checking his apartment would be a good idea. However, we do not have a key."

"It's a missing persons investigation. Getting a warrant shouldn't be difficult, especially since it's been more than a month that he's been missing. Tope, you want to go take care of the warrant? You may have to get help from the captain, as Smithville isn't part of our sandbox."

"I'll take care of it." Tope stood and nodded to Grant and Shannon. "It's good to meet you both. We'll get this figured out, Shannon. No one's better at finding people than Grant, from what Sawyer has told me. However, Sawyer lies, so…"

"Will you get out of here?" Sawyer threw a pencil at Tope, who ducked as he rushed out the door.

"You should be more careful, cousin. You could put an eye out doing that," Grant teased.

"Oh, right, like you know. There are other ways to put an eye out that are much more…efficient. If I wanted to take his eye, I could." A sarcastic grin spread across his face.

"You two are kind of dangerous together," laughed Shannon. "I'm not sure this is such a good idea."

"It's a good idea, alright," said Sawyer. "I relish the opportunity to work again with that man." Sawyer pointed at Grant.

"Aw, cousin, you flatter me," Grant said, his eyes sparkling with mischief. "Say that slower, enunciate well."

The room erupted in laughter and the three rose.

"What do you say we head over to the Rank and File and grab some lunch?" Sawyer slapped his cousin on the back as they went to meet Tope. Grant held out his hand to Shannon. She quickly grabbed it and moved in beside him. Grant could almost feel the smirk Sawyer was fighting to keep from his lips…again.

A popular law enforcement hang out, the Rank and File Tavern also had some of the best food in town. Sawyer, Tope, Grant and Shannon found Sawyer's familiar seat by the window.

"Cousin," smiled Grant, "why have they not put a plaque with your name on it in this booth?"

"They keep telling me that they're going to do that," replied Sawyer, returning the sarcasm, "but I always tell them no, that I don't want them to go to any special effort just for me."

"You don't have to worry about that, Sawyer," laughed Tope. "They won't."

The waitress came and took their orders and Grant returned to the issue at hand, that of finding Jimmy Norton.

"I know this is your jurisdiction Sawyer, so you tell me how you want to handle this investigation."

"First of all, you're having dinner with Esley and I tonight, both of you," he said nodding to Shannon.

"Hey, what about me?" protested Tope. "I like to eat dinner. And *nobody* cooks a dinner like Esley."

"You're always invited, Tope. That goes without saying." Sawyer got a slightly panicked look on his face. "I really should let Es know you're coming."

Sawyer rose and pulled his cell phone from his pocket, looking for a place where he could talk and be heard. The Rank and File tended to get a little noisy this time of the day.

"Hey, Es. How would you feel about company for dinner?"

Chapter Thirteen

When the group arrived for dinner, a very pregnant Esley was waiting with food on the table. As was usually the case, Esley was the perfect hostess-on-the-fly. Tope had stopped at his home and picked up Camille, his wife. It was obvious Esley and Camille were good friends. They chatted and laughed, inviting Shannon into their conversation and explaining the jokes as they went. Shannon was quiet, but joined in a little bit with the women. Grant was happy to see her interacting and relaxing a little bit.

Dinner was delicious, and afterward the group sat in the living room and watched baby Jack play, bringing toys to everyone to examine and play with. Baby Jack was three years old now, and they called him "JB" which was the abbreviation of his namesake, Jack Baker. Jack Baker was Sawyer's partner for many years prior to his murder just over three years ago.

"There's my little man," laughed Tope, throwing the boy into the air. The room was filled with JB's giggles and screams as Tope caught him and tossed him into the air again. "Are you being a good boy?" He caught JB and set him in the crook of his arm.

"I *always* a good boy," smiled JB as he gazed admiringly at Tope. "Mommy says so."

"And you will learn that mommy is *always* right," laughed Tope. He set the little one gently onto the floor and JB scooped up several different toy trucks and cars and made his way to Grant.

"Dis is my birfday twuck," said JB, displaying it proudly in the air. "And dis one is my best caow. It's Daddy's wook caow." This time he was holding up a police cruiser. "My daddy is a po-weece-man." He continued on through the remainder of the cars and trucks, describing each one and what its function was in his world.

"JB," began Grant with a smile, "you are a talker like your father."

The boy beamed and crawled up into Grant's lap. "Dis is my best twuck," he said. "Santa bwought it to ouh house foh Chwistmas." He proudly displayed the truck for all to see.

Once he finished introducing the group to his toys, JB played quietly in the middle of the room as the adults visited around him.

"Sawyer neglected to tell us you were expecting a little one, and soon, I would guess," said Grant with a smile. "If he had, we would have gone out to eat and not put you out like we have. Just for that, Sawyer will do the dishes."

Esley laughed and cuddled into Sawyer who was sitting beside her. "I was going to crack that whip once everyone left. He's not getting away with *this*. There are consequences for such actions. He *must* be punished." Her eyes twinkled as she squeezed his hand.

As the evening continued on, Shannon became quiet, watching the group interact. Grant decided it was time to call it a night and get Shannon home. They said their goodbyes, and the two of them strolled quietly to Shannon's SUV.

She stopped at the front of the car and leaning on the hood, said softly, "Jimmy's out there somewhere, Grant, and he's alone. I know he needs me, I know he is either waiting for me to come and find him, or he's in some kind of trouble and he doesn't want me to know about it."

Grant moved closer and put his arms around Shannon, hugging her. "It is a very big world when you search for one person, especially one person who you love and care about. I know it feels very overwhelming right now, but you are not alone. I am here, and so are Sawyer and Tope. We will all work together and we will find him. Stay strong. Do not give up hope."

Grant opened the passenger door and waited for Shannon to climb in. He came around the front of the car to the drivers side and slid into the seat. He spoke as he put the keys in the ignition and started the car.

"The search warrant will allow us to get the key to Jimmy's apartment from the manager of the units. Hopefully we will get some idea of where he has gone, or what he has gotten himself into. Sawyer is meeting us in Smithville tomorrow at your apartment. We will go to Jimmy's from there."

Shannon nodded and said nothing. She was silent for a while then spoke. "I can't help but think that Jimmy has gotten involved in something that he can't get out of. It's just this nagging feeling that, whatever it is, he's in over his head. I feel a sense of urgency, like he's running out of time, which means *we're* running out of time. It makes my stomach churn."

"You must keep your mind focused on finding him, not on what he is experiencing or not experiencing. This is not an easy thing to do, but you must do it. Keep your mind focused on Jimmy and nothing else. The Spirits will be able to guide you then, and only then. This is important."

"Yes, but easier said than done," said Shannon with a deep sigh. "But I'll try."

"That is all that matters."

They arrived at Shannon's apartment that evening about ten o'clock. She turned the key in the lock and gasped as the door opened. She hadn't turned on the lights, but she could tell her apartment had been ransacked. She reached from the outside hallway, through the doorway to the light switch, and Grant could then see what had caused her reaction.

"I take it your home does not always look like this," he said, trying to reduce the tension.

"I…I…" Shannon gasped again as she peeked around the now open door. Grant's attempt had done nothing for her tension level. "Who would do something like this?"

Grant took her shoulders and gently moved her, placing him between Shannon and the rest of the apartment. "Wait here. Let me check the rooms first."

"I'm not standing out here by myself," she said firmly. "I'm staying with you."

"Then stay behind me."

The two of them moved slowly through the small apartment and found that no one was there. Shannon relaxed a little once they found the house was empty, but she stared at the mess as though she was in someone else's apartment and seeing it for the first time.

"We had better call the police. Don't touch anything, Shannon. We will see what the police have to say."

Grant quickly dialed 911 and within a few minutes there were sirens coming down the street. The cruisers rolled up to the front of the apartment complex and proceeded to Shannon's apartment per Grants directions.

Shannon let the officers into her apartment and the usual questions were asked. "Have you noticed any strangers in the neighborhood? Have you seen anyone in the building that didn't belong there? Have you noticed you were being followed home at any time?"

Shannon was exasperated at the last question.

"I filed a missing persons report for my brother. I haven't seen him for more than a month now. When I filed the report, I also mentioned that I felt I was being followed. I had seen SUVs following me and they were often parked outside my building. I've told you this already."

The officer was patient with her. He responded kindly. "I'm sorry about your brother. I will check the report and add this incident to it. Is there anything missing?"

"I…I don't know. We didn't want to touch anything until you'd inspected it."

"We've done about all we can do, but if you find something *is* missing, please call the department and let them know this is in connection with a filed missing persons report." He added tentatively, "I know this has been upsetting for you, but we need to get your fingerprints so we can see if there are any that don't belong."

Shannon submitted to the finger printing and when it was finished, the officers filed out of the apartment and Shannon used the wet wipe they'd given her to shut the door. She stood still, staring at the doorknob like she was expecting it to tell her something, mindlessly wiping the ink from her finger tips.

Grant put his arm around her shoulders. "Here," he said, picking up a sofa cushion and placing it on the sofa. "Sit down. I think you need to process some things."

Shannon appeared numb. In the last week she'd flown to Alaska, been privy to a shooting where someone was killed, found out she'd been followed all the way to Alaska, her rental car was bombed, and now she was home again, only to find her home had been ransacked. For what purpose? Prior to all of this, her brother had disappeared without a trace. It did not surprise Grant to see that her mind was beginning to shut down. He was certain she had to be feeling there was no more room for thinking. Her eyes took on a vacant look of someone who's brain felt stuffed with unanswered questions.

Grant could see the despair forming. "Shannon, listen to me." He took the wet cloth from her hands and put it on the coffee table.

Shannon lifted her head, her dark eyes bored into Grant. His stomach jumped at the beauty and depth of those eyes, but he forced himself to think of her, and how she was feeling.

"You've been through more in the last month than most people endure in their lifetimes." He knelt before her and took her hands in his. "This is going to take some adjusting, and I want to help you do that. Tell me how you are feeling."

Shannon shook her head softly and gazed around at what had once been a neatly kept home. "I don't know what to tell you. I'm numb. I just…I'm numb."

"That is a good place to start. Numbness wears off, and this will, too. Take the time you need to process what you are seeing and what you have seen."

Eventually Shannon stood and surveyed the room. She slowly began picking up things in the living room and put them back in their proper place. Grant helped by picking up the remaining cushions and replacing them on the couch and chairs. They continued through the apartment, room by room, until everything was back in its place.

"Nothing seems to be missing," said Shannon, inspecting each room's contents. "But I have no idea what they were looking for. I can't think I'd have anything that anyone would even want."

Grant looked around at the now tidy apartment. "We should get some sleep. It is past midnight and you need rest."

Shannon was frowning, her brow shooting downward; her mouth was a thin line, and her eyes flashed angrily. In seconds the anger changed to a look of stubborn determination. "I'll help you make the guest room bed. Let me go get the clean linens."

"Wait. Shannon, wait," Grant touched her arm softly and she stopped. "Just breathe. I am fine. I can make my own bed. You, however, need to think, and breathe and then breathe some more. Move slowly; relax your shoulders. Do not let those who did this take any more from you."

Shannon's dark eyes widened as an understanding seemed to creep across her face, a realization of what Grant was saying.

Grant helped the feeling along. "You said you felt like you were losing yourself in this process of finding Jimmy. You must allow your 'self,' your 'soul,' to aid in this investigation, and for that to happen you must think slowly through things and remember to breathe." Grant's tone was deep and soothing. His eyes reached into her and touched a familiar string in her heart.

The even, dark tone of her skin returned and Shannon's eyes softened. "I know what you just did," she said. "You wanted me to calm down so the Spirits could help me process what has just happened in my home. And they did that. I'm not frightened anymore. You can help me make your bed." Her smile was soft, a little forced, but it was a smile. She was breathing.

"You must get some rest. I am a big boy…I can make my own bed."

Shannon ignored his comment and led Grant down the hall to the first door. "I'll get the linens," she said. "They're in the linen closet in the bathroom."

She returned quickly and they made up the bed. Once the last blanket was laid out and straightened into place, Shannon stood and ran her hand through her long black hair with a sigh. "I don't remember ever being so frustrated. But I know what you're going to say. 'We will find him.' I know you're right, but I feel like I'm on a treadmill, going nowhere as fast as I can."

"I understand. You need to rest, Shannon. I can see it in your eyes. You are exhausted, and we have much work to do. Your brain needs sleep, right along with the rest of you."

"I know," she replied. The fatigue was heavy in her voice. "You're right. We'll talk more in the morning. Just don't be expecting a breakfast like the ones you prepared for me in Alaska." Her eyes softened with a smile.

Grant chuckled. "Maybe I can help. It is the least I can do."

"Good luck finding anything. I haven't been shopping for a while."

"Sleep now. We will worry about breakfast in the morning."

Shannon left the guest room, closing the door behind her. With all the activities of the day, Grant had very little time that morning for meditation and he could feel the call of his soul, needing the time for quiet contemplation. He found a corner of the room and sat quietly on the floor with his legs folded in front of him and his hands resting palm up on each knee.

Grant felt the release of the day's tension as he cleared his mind and chased away the concerns of the day. The peace was welcomed, and he knew he would sleep that night.

After several minutes, Grant rose and lay down on the bed. He'd become accustomed to sleeping in his clothes, knowing Shannon might need company in order to sleep. He found himself chuckling softly. *I will never understand this feeling. I know you spoke to me, Mother, of love and companionship, but your wisdom is far from what I feel. Help me now understand these emotions. I will need your strength."*

The thought had not more than entered his brain when there was the familiar knock on the guest room door. The door opened softly and Shannon slipped into the room carrying an extra blanket.

"It's a little scary out there," she said. "Do you mind?"

"No, I do not mind." Grant rose from the bed and turned down the covers for her.

"You don't have to do that, I brought a blanket," she said, holding it out for him to see.

Grant took the blanket from her. "I will use the blanket, you sleep under the covers."

The muted moonlight through the window blinds shown softly on her baby blue silk pajamas. The color accented her smooth skin and dark hair, making her eyes seem bigger and darker. She was beautiful, more beautiful than any living thing that he could recall.

Shannon slid under the covers and turned to face Grant's side of the bed. He sighed and lay down beside her.

"We've got to stop meeting like this," she said with a rye smile.

"I am becoming rather accustomed to it," he chuckled. "This could get to be a habit, you know."

"Not if you're living in Alaska and I'm in Iowa."

Grant sighed and closed his eyes, unsure of his feelings and if they would betray him. "Sleep now."

"I will if you will," she teased.

"I will," he said firmly, more to convince himself than anyone else.

Chapter Fourteen

The next morning Shannon awoke to the familiar smell of hot coffee and food cooking. She wondered if she'd been magically transported back to Alaska, mostly because her kitchen never smelled that good.

She stood and stretched as she walked to the door and opened it. The aromas from her kitchen were even stronger and she followed her nose down the hallway.

Grant was in his element. He had a kitchen towel tucked into the waist of his pants and he was turning hash browns onto a plate to place in a warmed oven.

"Where did you find this stuff?" she asked. "I had hash browns?"

"In your freezer," he chuckled. "And your eggs were fairly fresh. You must have bought them shortly before you left for Alaska."

Shannon sat down at the table. "I don't even remember."

"We will eat breakfast. Sawyer called and he and Tope will be here in about an hour. Will you be able to meet with them? If not, I can do it and you can rest."

"That's very kind, Grant. But I need to hear what is said. I also wanted to let you know that I will need to go back to work on Monday. My time off is quickly becoming extinct. I don't want to use it all up, in case I need it for…for a funeral. I can't pay rent or buy food without my job. So, back to work I go."

Somehow Grant knew her return to work would be for the best. Being around Shannon was making it more and more difficult for him to think. He needed all of his gifts for this investigation, for Shannon. He knew he would…miss her. That was a new feeling for him. He would miss her.

"We must not be thinking about funerals unless it is absolutely necessary. Until we know different, Jimmy is alive and missing. That is all. Maybe work will help keep your mind on other things. Just know, I will handle this Shannon; with the help of Sawyer and Tope we will find Jimmy. I will keep you apprised of what is found each day."

They cleaned up the breakfast dishes and wiped down the table. Shannon was deep in thought.

"I believe they will be here soon," said Grant as they went into the living room.

The words had no more than left his lips when there was a knock at the door.

Shannon jumped and Grant motioned for her to move further down her hallway from the kitchen. He stood against the wall, next to the door.

"Who is there?"

"It's Sawyer. I have Tope with me."

Grant opened the door to a wary Sawyer. "What's happened? You're being awfully covert." Sawyer's head moved from side to side as he spoke, searching.

"Someone went through Shannon's home while she was gone. It was a disaster when we arrived. We cleaned it up last night when we got here, after the police left."

"You did call the police, then? Good. They probably checked for fingerprints."

Grant nodded in the affirmative and Tope gave voice to Grant's thoughts. "There won't be any fingerprints, Sawyer. I'd be willing to bet on that."

"The police came quickly, but they found nothing. They are checking now for fingerprints of unknown origin. And yes, I doubt they will find any that don't belong here."

Grant motioned for both men to come in. Shannon returned from the hallway and the four of them sat down in the living room. Sawyer was the first to speak. "I talked with Captain Amerson this morning and we got our search warrant for Jimmy's apartment. We also got his approval to work this case with you, but we are to keep him informed, and you know what that means."

The three men said the word at the same time. "Reports."

"Sorry, Cousin, but those will be *your* doing. I have no jurisdiction here." Grant sighed with mock disappointment. "However, I will help where I can."

Sawyer tossed him a knowing nod. "*Right*, you will. I'm sure we'll be able to find a few forms for you to 'fill in.' "

Shannon watched the three of them, this time with interest. Her earlier tension was long past and

Grant felt relaxation and amusement from her. It reminded her of how she and Jimmy would tease each other and there was an instant tug at her heartstrings. She tried to ignore it, but the memories had a way of forcing their way in and insisting that you watch the movie as it played in her mind.

The three men continued sending jabs back and forth and Shannon was caught up in the memories of her brother, paying little attention to the men.

Hey, Shan...let's skip school and drive to the beach today. It's sunny and even warm! Not often we get those two elements in the same Alaska Spring day. Jimmy's voice was clear and clean, innocent. His eyes sparkled and his smile was instantly contagious. She always did have a hard time telling him no. But his grades were falling, and she was the only one who seemed to be able to corral him back into current tasks. Today, however, was different. The day truly was beautiful, and even she felt it was ridiculous to stay inside. So, unlike her usual stance, she caved and they were off to the beach. She loved listening to him speak of girls that he was attracted to, of teachers he couldn't stand and tricks he and his friends would play on each other. How she loved her brother.

"Looks like we're boring her, but she must like it. She's certainly smiling big enough." Tope was watching her; in fact all three were watching her as she felt herself pulled back into the present.

"Nonsense. I was simply observing that you three have an interesting way of interacting with each other," she said, still smiling. "I'm sure you'll all work together very efficiently. Now, shall we head over to Jimmy's apartment? It's not far from here."

Grant chuckled. "Very well." He knew her though, and he knew she was somewhere else when they were talking. However, he also knew it was a good memory, and he was happy to let her keep it to herself.

They drove down the street, not far from Shannon's complex, and hurried inside out of the cold, biting wind. Knocking first at the manager's apartment, they showed the older woman the search warrant and she excused herself to get the keys. She returned, keys in hand, and they made their way to Jimmy's apartment. But when the door was opened, Shannon was, once again, not prepared for what she would find there.

Chapter Fifteen

The beautifully furnished room looked like something out of a home living magazine. Beautiful furnishings and exquisite décor whispered to her of success and accomplishment. It wasn't that she thought her brother unsuccessful, but she had to ask the question.

"You're certain this is Jimmy Norton's apartment?" Shannon stared at the landlady with dark, unbelieving eyes.

"Young lady," she replied, with obvious indignity, "I think I *know* what renter has which apartment. You will see that I have retrieved his mail. His mailbox was overflowing and I was asked in a notice from the postal service to empty it. I have done that. It's all there, on the table. Unopened. I *know* which tenant is which, what apartment they occupy and I take good care of them when they are away."

Grant cleared his throat. "I am sorry Mrs…"

"Jeanine. My name is Jeanine."

"I am sorry Jeanine, for the misunderstanding. May I ask, is Jimmy's rent up to date?"

"As it always is," she said, then, continuing thoughtfully, "Although, last month, and then again this month, his rent came in the mail. Cash as usual, but with only a sticky note that had his name and apartment number on it. I left the receipt for payment on the kitchen table with the mail." She pointed into the kitchen with obvious pride in her own thoughtfulness. "Jimmy is a sweet boy. He told me, if I ever needed to get into his apartment when he wasn't here, that I had his permission."

"Thank you, Jeanine. We appreciate your help, and your patience." Grant motioned to the door. Once she was gone he closed the door and Grant, Sawyer, and Tope all waited for Shannon to explain.

Not realizing the silence in the room was on her account, Shannon came out of her stupor and turned to see the three men staring at her, waiting for her to speak.

"Oh, sorry…I…I just always thought Jimmy didn't want me in here because he didn't have nice things, which was a stupid reason, but I respected his privacy. I see I was a little off on that assumption."

Shannon scanned the room, unable to do anything but stare at the lavish décor. The entry held beautiful, expensive leather furniture. The matched set included a couch, and two recliners. Nice end tables with beautiful ornate lamps sat on either end of the sofa.

"Grant, I know Jimmy, and I know he didn't have the income to support these kinds of purchases. Yet, for all his time gone," Shannon was at the table, leafing through the mail, "I don't see any bills, or late notices. How could this be…" Her voice trailed off.

"Let's have a look around," said Sawyer. "Tope and I will take the bedroom."

The group split up and Grant stayed with Shannon in the living room and kitchen area. Shannon wasn't over her shock yet, and spoke with still stunned surprise. She'd been walking around the table as she spoke and came upon what looked like a real estate contract of some kind. "Grant, is this what I think it is? He was buying a *house*?" There was a set of keys lying beside the form.

Grant had found nothing out of the ordinary in the living room and hurried to Shannon's side. "Let me see," he said, reading the first page carefully. "Yes, he was certainly buying a house. Actually, to be more exact, he *bought* a house," said Grant, leafing through the pages of the contract. "And he paid cash for it."

"He *what?*"

"However, I do not think the house was for him."

Grant let his words sink in slowly. Shannon was quickly becoming overwhelmed with what she'd seen and heard so far.

"Then...who was the house for?" Her voice dripped with uncomfortable suspicion.

"Sit down. Let me review this with you."

Shannon sat down at the table beside Grant and he pointed to the name on the contract. "He bought the home for you, Shannon. It looks like he closed on it before he disappeared." Grant picked up the set of keys from the table. "I am fairly certain these keys are your house keys."

A call came from the bedroom. "Hey you two, I found something." The voice was Tope's. Shannon's large eyes briefly searched Grant's face. He set the contract and the keys back on the table and helped Shannon out of her chair. They hurried into the bedroom.

Tope and Sawyer stood in front of a low, wide chest of drawers with a large mirror on top. In Tope's hand there was a business-sized card, plain white with only a handwritten number on it. The number appeared to be a telephone number.

"This card smacks of FBI involvement. If I were guessing, Jimmy was an informant for the FBI. Did he ever talk about the FBI, like he wanted to work for them one day, or even that he was interested in them?"

"Never. He loved his job; he was happy to be doing just what he was doing. He always said that."

Shannon left the three men and went to Jimmy's closet. She found expensive suits and shirts hanging there, leather shoes on the floor and high-end silk ties on a fancy, mechanical rotating tie holder. Her brain struggled to make sense of everything she saw. This was not the Jimmy she knew.

"When I was with the FBI," said Tope, "these were the sort of cards they passed out to informants. The informant would call the number on the card, say only the name of the agent they wanted the information to go to, and then give them the information, briefly, or possibly a place to meet so he could then give them the information in person."

Tope stared at the card and pulled out his cell phone. "I'm gonna try something…" he said as he dialed the number.

The phone rang and Tope began to speak. "This is Jimmy Norton, I-" The call was terminated. "Okay," smiled Tope, "that is definitely FBI. But let me check one more thing."

He dialed the same number again and a voice came on the line saying the number he was calling was not a valid number and to please try the number again.

"Just as I thought. When there is a breach in protocol, the number is immediately, and I mean *immediately* terminated."

Shannon collapsed onto the end of the bed in a stupor, sitting up, mumbling to herself.

"He couldn't afford these clothes, the furniture, a *house*, he could barely afford his apartment. Jimmy was a jeans and t-shirt guy, second hand at that. The same was true of his shoes. This can't be his apartment. It can't be. FBI? Cash for real estate? This can't be his home. No way. We're in the wrong apartment."

Shannon stood as if she were going to march right down the hall and give that landlady a piece of her mind. Grant stood in front of her and took her hand.

"Remember what I said? Breathe, Shannon. Just breathe your way through this. You will not find your brother by ignoring what you see, no matter how unreal it appears. Accept what your eyes are telling you, and let your brain absorb what you see. It is important if you want to help Jimmy."

Shannon searched Grant's dark eyes. It felt to him as if she could see all the way to the back of his head.

"Breathe, Shannon. Take a big deep breath." Grant helped her out to the living room and sat with her on the couch.

As they left, Tope turned to Sawyer. "Who is this guy? He talks like some kind of religious sage or something."

"In a way, he is," said Sawyer. "That's my cousin, and if you ever heard him talk to a horse, you'd know he speaks no differently to animals than he does to people. He's like a giant walking heart."

"*A what*? Has it ever occurred to you he might be a little weird? You're not going stupid on me, are you?"

Sawyer elbowed his partner and went into the living room. Tope left the room muttering under his breath. "I've heard of family dysfunction, but this is over the top. The guy talks to horses? A giant walking heart? Right."

Grant and Shannon were deep in conversation as Sawyer and Tope entered the room. "I just don't understand any of this, Grant. Where did this furniture come from? He paid *cash* for a house, and it's for *me*? Where is he getting his money?"

"I still have a contact at the FBI," said Tope, studying the business card. He glanced at his watch and made a mental note of the time difference between Iowa and Washington, D.C. "Let me make a phone call tomorrow and see if he can tell me anything I don't already know about this card."

The group had spent nearly the whole day in Jimmy's apartment. They'd searched every corner, drawer and cabinet. Sawyer couldn't believe they hadn't even stopped for lunch.

"Where did the time go? I can't believe it's this late. It feels like we just got here.

Grant's concern for Shannon was growing. "What do you say we call it a day?"

Everyone agreed and Grant took Shannon back to her apartment.

As they entered the apartment, Grant could sense a feeling of fear emanating from her. She was losing her strength and power to fatigue.

"You need rest, Shannon. Come, sit. Relax for a minute before you go to bed."

"No, you have to be hungry. I'm afraid I don't have much to offer, but at least I could get you a sandwich or something."

"You have done enough. If I get hungry, I will make myself a sandwich. Sit down. Relax for a minute."

Grant helped her to the couch and sat down beside her.

Shannon laid her head on his shoulder and they sat in comfortable silence for several minutes. As Shannon's breathing slowed, Grant could tell she was beginning to fall asleep. He nudged her gently and stood.

"Shannon, you are ready for sleep. Let me help you to your room."

Putting up no fight to his suggestion, Shannon muttered half asleep, "It's like I never have to explain how I'm feeling to you because you already know. How do you do that?"

Not requiring an answer, she allowed Grant to help her to her room. . Nearly unable to lift her feet off the floor, they moved slowly down the hallway. Leaving her clothed, he turned down the covers and helped her into bed. She was almost asleep before her head landed gently on the pillow. Grant leaned over her and studied the beautiful face for a moment. He lowered his face to hers and kissed her softly on the forehead, then he turned quickly, walked to her door, and switched off her light.

Grant turned off the lights in the rest of the apartment and entered the guest room. He lay in the darkness thinking through the information they'd gathered during the search of Jimmy's apartment. There was much to think about, including his belongings, apparently so much more expensive than the Jimmy his sister knew. It was the same with the furnishings, and then there was the house purchase.

Grant felt Jimmy had fallen head first into a dangerous situation with no way to get out. There was something in the pit of his soul that made him uncomfortable. Something he was either missing, or not seeing at all.

Shannon's presence had thrown him off his game somewhat, and he couldn't let that happen. It was a fox chasing its tail. She'd come to him for help, but his feelings for her were skewing his view, his instincts. When she was in the room, any room, her presence filled his senses with…a different kind of life than he'd ever experienced before. How was he to separate Shannon from the search for her brother? It was like separating conjoined twins. Sometimes it couldn't be done, but sometimes it could. He would make it work for Shannon. He would need more help from the Spirits than ever before, but he knew with their help, he could accomplish what Shannon needed from him.

Was she aware of the impact she'd made in his life? Grant fell asleep with that thought floating in his head and dreamed again of ravens and eagles, soaring through the skies together, dipping and climbing, intertwining in ways that made him ache. It seemed with the raven at his side, the eagle could climb higher, fly faster, see clearer. All was as it should be in the dream. All was as it should be.

Chapter Sixteen

Jimmy Norton walked slowly down the street, his collar up to keep the cold wind off his neck, his hat pulled down over his dark hair. Coal dark eyes searched the street and its shops. There were people around him, but not many. All of them were too busy to notice him, and those that did wanted no part of him. His mind wandered through layers of guilt, as it usually did, and his thoughts came to rest on his sister, as *they* usually did.

He should have told her he wasn't coming for breakfast that day. In the months prior to that no show, he should have told her he was hooked on cocaine and alcohol again. She would have helped him. Knowing Shannon, she was looking for him, and he prayed she wouldn't look where she shouldn't. He couldn't warn her, didn't dare. If he called her, and they discovered the call, which they would, they'd use her as a weapon to keep him doing their bidding. He'd seen it happen all too often, and though he'd made no overtures of leaving the organization, they liked to have that ace in the hole when needed.

These people must never know he had a sister. In the back of that thought rested the realization that he was glad his parents had already passed from this life. At least *they* were safe and would never know the awful things he'd done.

Safe. Was anyone safe? He was now equally as feared as those he worked for, and he hated it.

He continued walking, constantly checking his position, making sure he wasn't being followed. Jimmy was tall and slender in his long wool coat, a picture of good breeding. The thought made him want to wretch right there on the sidewalk.

The desire to run from the organization who'd adopted him with such kindness, was strong of late. In the beginning they'd been so good to him, taken him in like one of their own. But it wasn't long before orders were given and he was expected to comply or be eliminated. The scope of those orders had been so gradual in the beginning, moving from special deliveries to the issuing of threats for nonpayment of contracts, then moving on to using bombs to destroy property and then the killing of those who refused to comply with the organizations demands. Looking back, it seemed like quite the leap from delivery boy to murderer, but somehow, when he was in the middle of it, it all seemed so logical…so…normal.

He'd first come upon these people while working with the FBI as an informant. The thought made him laugh. Informant. What a complete waste of time. They paid him pennies to risk his life finding out information on the same people who'd later hired him for menial deliveries and paid him exorbitant amounts of money. The move was an easy one, from FBI to the organization.

In retrospect, however, it didn't seem so easy. Now he wished for a hole so deep that he could jump in and pull the earth in over him. It was too late, though. He'd sunk too far into the family's business for that now. He belonged to them. He'd become their robot. They programmed his instructions and he did as he was told. Hate. It was the only word that formed in his drug dependent brain now. He killed to stay alive, but was this existence worth staying alive for?

The idea that they called themselves family made him want to wretch. *The Family.* Not like any family he'd ever been part of. Why didn't he see that from the beginning? What was wrong with him? These people were no family to him. He was nothing more than a means to an end.

He'd beat drugs and alcohol once. He reminded himself of this often, and told his brain that when he had enough money stashed away he'd get off his dependency again, just like he had before. But he had to have the drugs now to numb himself from the horrible things he did, and that cost money.

Jimmy slowed his walk to a stroll, then stopped as he came to an intersection and peered around the corner before turning and heading down the sidewalk. In the midday light, he saw the shop owner sweeping the walk in front of his store. The shopkeeper was completely unaware he'd signed his own death warrant by turning down the Brevet's offer to buy his establishment. It wasn't even that, so much, as the fact that he'd turned them into the police. Unheard of! Didn't he know who they were? By the next morning the man would be dead. His shop and the home he kept above it would be decimated.

The young killer watched his own image in store windows as he continued down the sidewalk. An empty shell, barely human in itself, was all that remained of the once gentle, good and kind Jimmy Norton. The thought brought a shiver as he shrugged deeper into his coat.

He wore nice clothes now; the coat was expensive and warmed him well. But to have these nice things, he was forced into obedience, like a trained dog, doing what he needed to do to be "fed," and he was well fed. This life was what he'd always dreamed of having; power, class, control. He laughed at that last thought. The one thing he *wasn't,* was in control, but at least he had the other things. He had lots of nice things now.

Jimmy strolled casually by the shop owner, tipping his hat and smiling at the man. The man returned the smile, and having finished his task, stepped back inside the shop. Jimmy's eyes grew cold, like ice, as he plotted the evening's work he would do. And he would do it, because that was who he'd become.

Only a few months ago, he was holding down a job and trying to make ends meet, but happy with the life he had. He'd bought a handgun, only for the sport of target shooting, and he'd spent every Saturday, once breakfast with Shannon was done, at the shooting range, learning to use his new toy. Sometimes he would go in the evenings after work, just to get in a few extra hours of practice.

It was on one of those evenings he was approached by a nicely dressed man, a *very* nicely dressed man. The man complimented Jimmy on his shooting. He asked how long he'd been target practicing and he seemed honestly surprised at how proficient young Jimmy had become in such a short time. For the following weeks, the man showed him how to fine-tune his stance, his grip, and his pull on the trigger.

That was when the FBI agent approached him. The agent asked him, in so many words, what his new friend had said. Jimmy promptly told him what he talked about with his friends was none of his business, and that landed him with a bag over his head in a small conference room somewhere in town where he was threatened with prison time for fraternizing with known criminals. Jimmy was told the only way he could stay out of prison, was to report to his new FBI "Handler" each week with what his friend said to him, and what this new friend asked Jimmy to do for him.

That seemed like years ago now, though it had only been a few months. Often Jimmy and his friend would meet up at the local tavern after those evening target practices, becoming friends with a shared interest in shooting.

Since his rehab, Jimmy had steered clear of alcohol, but when he was with this man, he felt he could control the drinking, and was certain he wouldn't allow it to get the better of him. Before long, the two were drinking together like old friends, calling each other "Buddy" or "Bud." Any time Jimmy asked him his name, and the man had said, "Just call me Buddy. That works for me." So he became Buddy. And soon, without Jimmy realizing what was happening, he was drinking, and he was drinking a *lot*.

Somehow, and at some time in those weeks together, the boy who prided himself on being Shannon's brother had been talked into trying some drugs that Buddy used. If this man could live the life he was living and do drugs like he did, surely it wouldn't harm *Jimmy* to try them. What had *really* happened was the end of Jimmy Norton, and the beginning of whatever soul-dead animal he'd become. He was using drugs and drinking even while he was meeting Shannon every Saturday morning for breakfast. Shannon never noticed, probably because she would never believe it of him. She was the one who helped him out of his addiction the first time. She not only trusted him, she'd had complete faith in him. Jimmy shuddered and his step quickened.

And then there was Raina. They'd been seeing each other for more than a year, spending lots of time together in the evenings after work, at least until he met up with his new friend. It was only in the last few weeks with Raina that he began to see how difficult it was to hide anything from her. The last time he was her, his rudeness and his words were cruel, even beyond cruel. He wanted her to stay away from him, for her own safety, and in so doing, he'd said things he never wanted to remember. She was the one person in his life he *couldn't* think about. His shame in lying about his life to his sister was bad enough, but his actions with Raina were unforgiveable.

At first it was easy to hide his second life. However, soon, Jimmy decided he needed to do things more covertly. His relationship with Raina was kept hidden, even from the guys at the shop, and especially from his sister. He had to keep Shannon and Raina separate, as together they made a bigger target, and the organization liked bigger targets.

He was able to report what he was doing to the FBI agent each week and tell them what he'd been asked to do while holding onto a job and making his life look normal. However, as time went on, it became more of a struggle, until one day he needed a hit more than he needed breakfast with his sister, more than he needed Raina and the love she offered him, and more than he needed to keep himself out of prison. And at that point, he belonged to the organization, and the weekly meetings with the FBI stopped.

Those early days of easy deliveries for the organization were seemingly harmless. Each delivery would net him more money than he'd make in a month at his job. Before long, he didn't even need the job anymore. The deliveries were paying far more than he'd ever thought possible.

It was like suddenly striking it rich, until "Buddy" told him he was going to have to start paying for the drugs he was using. Jimmy had no idea how expensive the drug was, but by this time, he *needed* it, and that need outweighed anything else in his life.

There were times he dreamed of his father. At least he thought it was a dream. His father would come to him and tell him to stop accepting the drugs, that the Spirits would help him if he could just find a way to help himself.

That was when he was offered his first real job. Buddy had a name, as it happened. But only a first name, and Jimmy was too high most of the time to care. Buddy's name was Hammer, and he told Jimmy to keep calling him Buddy. Jimmy was never to call him Hammer. From the look on his face when he gave the order, Jimmy knew better than to disobey that order, and he was fine with Buddy anyway.

Buddy rarely seemed to be affected by the drugs he gave to Jimmy. He also appeared to be unaffected by the alcohol as well, and that became more noticeable as time went on, but by the time he realized Hammer wasn't actually drinking and doing drugs with him, it was also too late. Jimmy no longer cared who drank with him, who snorted the cocaine with him, he needed both of them and if Hammer never used, it was no business of his. When Jimmy was told to kill a man, kill a whole family, the drugs had done their job, and he'd obeyed without question.

Now, as Jimmy strode by the shopkeeper and his small insignificant store, he wanted to shake the man. *Why can't you just do what they ask you to do? It's your fault you're going to die. It's your fault, and the fault of every other storeowner like you who is making me into this robot. If you'd just DO what is asked, I wouldn't have to kill you! You idiot!*

As much as he tried to justify his life in his own mind, his heart always brought him back to the truth. He'd caved. He'd given into the money, to the drugs that money would buy, and to the alcohol. He had nice things now and was more than comfortable in every way but his heart. His brain was perfectly comfortable with his life, his heart was not, and so he stopped listening to its constant tug, until one day, thanks to the drugs he used several times a day now, he felt nothing at all.

How had he let this happen to him again? How had he become this unthinking, unfeeling, uncaring shell that was once a good person? It was impossible to remember the goodness he'd once possessed. Now all he saw when he looked at his reflection in those store windows was evil. He wanted out. He was done.

But the question remained: *how* would he make that happen? How could he protect Shannon? If they hadn't already discovered he had a sister, they would. He needed a plan, but there was something going on in the organization that was sucking time right out of him. Something had happened, someone hadn't returned from a job, and there were lots of secret meetings, rumors, and whispers.

Come to think of it, Jimmy had not seen Hammer in more than a week. Hammer was his "boss" and gave him instructions for new jobs he was assigned. His most recent job, however, came from a different source, not Hammer. Now that he allowed his brain to actually *think* about that and process that information, Jimmy had a bad feeling about it.

Had something happened to Hammer? Had they killed him? Was Jimmy next? He would die without ever knowing why. It was, seriously, time to go.

His next step was how. How would he leave an organization that knew more about him than he knew himself? He had to find a place to get the drugs and alcohol out of his system, but that would be easier said than done. He was in big trouble, and he knew it. And if he was in trouble, so was Shannon.

Chapter Seventeen

The phone rang a couple times before the familiar voice of Tope's FBI buddy picked up.

"Tooms."

"Hey Zach, it's me, Tope. How's it going?"

"Wow! It's the old married man. How's the married life?"

"It's much better than I thought it would be," laughed Tope. "You should try it sometime."

"I just might," replied Zach with a smile in his voice. "Melissa and I are getting pretty serious."

"Really? You think you might take the plunge?"

"I…I don't know. Talking about it makes me nervous." Zach coughed and quickly changed the subject. "You didn't call to talk about my personal relationship, fortunately, so how can I help you?"

"Aw, ya big chicken. You'll be fine." Tope laughed and continued. "I have a question for you. Have you heard the name Jimmy Norton around your parts?"

The line was quiet for several seconds. Tope began to wonder if Zach had hung up. Zach finally responded, softly and evasively. "Why do you want to know?"

"He's missing," said Tope. "Why are you whispering?"

"Listen, Tope," he began, still speaking very softly. "My hands are tied on this one. I can't help you."

"Okay, so you *have* heard of him then?"

There was another extended silence on the line and Tope waited, hoping he wouldn't hang up.

"I can lose my job for this," he said. "Once I tell you this, we're *even*, you hear me? No more favors. I happen to like my job." From the scratching sound, probably from Zach's chin scraping the phone receiver, it was obvious Zach was looking around as he spoke. He was more than uncomfortable on this one, he was flat out nervous.

"I understand."

"The man you're asking about worked with the agency. That's all I can say."

The call ended abruptly, and without a goodbye, and Tope stood alone in the conference room, wondering what had just happened. He hoped his friend had actually hung up and wasn't caught divulging information he shouldn't. What he did say was enough to confirm Tope's suspicions. Jimmy Norton had been an informant for the FBI. Now his biggest concern was how to break the news to Shannon. She knew Tope *thought* Jimmy was an informant, but he was pretty certain she hadn't accepted that fact. She appeared to be wound pretty tight when it came to her brother.

With a furrowed brow, Tope left the conference room, deep in thought. When he entered Sawyer's office, Grant and Shannon hadn't arrived yet. He was grateful for the privacy.

Once he explained to Sawyer what was found, Tope got a blank stare from Sawyer. "And…?"

"Okay, I guess it's all in the wording. Zach said Jimmy was working *with* the FBI, not *for* the FBI. That makes it a sure bet he's informing for them."

"You're certain about this? You know he's an informant from just one word?"

"Couldn't be any more sure if it was written across the sky. The guy was working with the FBI, passing information to them, but my friend wouldn't say anything else. I have no idea who he was supposed to be watching, nor do I know how deep into it he was. But at least we have the 'what,' we just don't have the 'who, when, or where.' He could have been working out of New York for all I know. His apartment wasn't ransacked like Shannon's apparently was."

"So, basically what you're telling me is you got nuthin', right?"

"Well…sort of, but not really," explained Tope. We know he was informing for the FBI. That's at least *something*."

"Right," sighed Sawyer.

Grant and Shannon entered the room and both Sawyer and Tope greeted them with an over abundance of forced enthusiasm.

"Good morning," smiled Sawyer, his eyebrows almost up to his hairline.

"Did you have a good night?" asked Tope, grinning far bigger than was necessary for the greeting.

Grant and Shannon stared at them for a moment and Shannon looked at Grant. "Are they okay?"

Grant laughed. "They are rarely okay."

Shannon nodded. "I see. I'm going to use the bathroom. You deal with them."

This made Grant chuckle again and Shannon hurried out the door.

"She thinks you are both weird, but I know different," he said. "You have found something. What is it?"

Tope reviewed the conversation he'd had with Zach and waited to see if Grant would catch the meaning in the conversation.

"He said *with* the FBI? Not *for*? That is a definite indicator that Jimmy was or is an informant. That is not good. The fact that Shannon has not heard from him could be very bad. What do you think?"

"SEE?" said Tope to Sawyer. "*He* gets the significance."

Sawyer scoffed at Tope and turned to Grant. "I'm concerned about telling Shannon. Can she handle this? It's not good news."

"No," said Grant, "it is not good news. However, she has to be told it is no longer a possibility. We will tell her when she comes back."

"Oh no you don't," said Tope. "*We* won't tell her. *You'll* tell her."

Grant stared from Sawyer to Tope and began to laugh. "You are afraid of her! You two big burley detectives…well, okay…big detectives are afraid of Shannon? I should make you tell her just for that. I think she will be proud to know she is so intimidating."

"Who's intimidating?" asked Shannon as she strolled into the room. She tossed her coat across the chair in front of Sawyer's desk and waited for an answer.

Grant smirked and muffled a laugh. "It is not important. But we have some information for you that you need to know. Please, sit down."

Sawyer was seated behind his desk and Tope sat in the chair beside the desk. There were two chairs in front of the desk. Shannon took one of them and Grant took the other. Grant turned his chair so he could face Shannon, beside her, but not directly in front of her.

"What's happened?" she asked, her face draining of color.

"We know a little more than we knew before," said Grant, "Tope spoke with his contact at the FBI, and it gave us a little more information, but it is important and I want to make sure you know everything that I know."

"I appreciate that, Grant."

"We learned from Tope's friend, that it is a certainty that Jimmy is an informant for the FBI. Do you know what that means?"

Shannon's eyes were wide with fear. "I do know what it means, but it can't be true. He worked at an auto shop downtown. He walked to work. He wore jeans and t-shirts, he came to my house every Saturday morning for breakfast, he was a good person, he worked hard and paid his bills, he-" The panic in her voice was rising and Grant stopped her.

"Shannon, stop. Breathe. Look at me. Look in my eyes and think about where you are and who you are with. You have to *hear* what I *am* saying to you, not what you want me to say. The FBI confirmed this. Jimmy is, or at least he was, an informant for the FBI. You have to let that sink in, because we know it for a fact. But there are a lot of things we do not know. Tope's contact could not tell us anything more than the fact that he worked 'with' the FBI."

Shannon's hands were trembling and she let go of Grant and stared at her lap. "I'm trying to hear what you're saying, but it goes against everything I know about my brother."

Tope stepped into the conversation. "Shannon, being an informant isn't necessarily a bad thing. It can really help the authorities a lot with arrests and convictions. It can, however, be a…a dangerous thing."

Shannon stared at Tope. Grant could tell she'd found her emotional footing, and now she was going to want answers. "If he's not still an informant, then where is he?"

"There are a lot of answers to that question, Shannon. Some are good and some are not." Tope paused.

"Give me the bad first." Shannon's eyes were focused and quickly becoming angry.

"Worst case scenario is he could have been found out. But he could also have started working for the people he was informing on, which can happen. I believe, if Jimmy were dead, my friend would have told me that. The fact that he couldn't talk to me about Jimmy Norton, tells me it's an ongoing investigation. Best case is that he skipped town and is hiding out waiting for everything to cool down before he comes back. He may be hoping the whole thing will blow over."

"Where is he?" demanded Shannon.

Sawyer jumped in this time. "We have no way of knowing that. He could be anywhere. From here we have to go back to the people he worked with, to his friends and begin asking different questions than you may have asked them."

"Like what?" Shannon's determination was back and she was holding Grant's hand again, stroking the back of it gently with her thumb. She'd definitely calmed down.

"Like, did they see him hanging around with anyone they didn't know? Was he becoming secretive, uneasy? Did he stop coming around, and if so, when did that happen?"

Grant broke in with a question. "Before we left Alaska, you told me you had spoken with his associates at work. You mentioned one girl, Raina, I think. You said she acted strange, or that maybe you thought there was something she was not telling you."

A look of hope filled Shannon's face. "That's right. Raina. Even I could tell she wasn't telling me the whole story. She knew something. I know she knew something, but I didn't know how to find that out, short of beating it out of her."

Sawyer leaned forward in his chair, folding his hands on his desk. "Then I guess that's where we need to start first. He worked in Smithville, correct?"

"Yes, at an auto shop called Thrifty Auto Repair. He was good at his work. Everyone there liked him. He spoke of it often, and of the people he worked with."

"Then we'll start there," said Sawyer. "Let's get a move on and see how much ground we can cover in Smithville today."

They rose and filed out the door, heading to the parking area. They decided to take two cars, mostly so they could split up and cover more ground.

Grant helped Shannon into the SUV and this time Grant drove.

"You handled that very well."

"Thanks to you. That breathing thing really works, you know."

Grant smiled. "Yes, I know. I use it quite often."

Shannon gaped at him. "You're kidding me, right? You don't get upset. Ever."

Grant chuckled softly. "Not that anyone can see, anyway, because I *breathe*."

Shannon leaned back in her seat. "I wanna be like you when I grow up."

Chapter Eighteen

Once they all arrived in Smithville, they split up. Rather than all four of them descending on Raina, it was decided that Grant and Shannon would go to Thrifty Auto Repair, talk to Raina and possibly other employees. Sawyer and Tope would see what they could find out by asking around the neighborhood, in the complex where Jimmy lived, and see what they could find there. Although they had precious little to go on, but they would exhaust every avenue they had for the time being.

As Grant and Shannon entered the repair shot, Shannon didn't see Raina. She asked one of the other workers if Raina was in.

"Over there," he said, pointing to a bay where a car was parked. "See the feet coming out from under that Chevy? That's Raina."

"Thanks."

The two of them approached the car.

"Raina?"

A nice looking blonde woman rolled out from under the car on a creeper and stared up at the two of them.

"You're Jimmy's sister." Raina's hair was disheveled and grease smears covered her nose and a bit on one cheek. Even then, her large blue eyes were deep in color and they searched her questioners with some irritation. "I told you I don't know anything."

Grant stepped in. "May I help you up? We just have a few more questions. Sometimes a person may know more than they think they do. We will not keep you for more than a few minutes."

Raina sat up on the creeper and stood without aid, moving the creeper away so no one would step on it. "What do you want to know?"

Grant took the interview and began asking questions. Shannon waited quietly, leaning against a car in the next bay.

"Do you remember when Jimmy was last seen at work?"

"Not really, I just remember noticing he'd not been here in a while. That was probably a month or more ago. He'd been missing work for about a week at that time."

"Before he went missing, did you ever think he was acting abnormally? Not being himself?"

Raina eyed Grant with suspicion. "Maybe."

"How would you describe the changes?"

"He was…happier. He seemed excited about life, like he'd won the lottery or something. Just before he stopped coming to work, he ordered pizza for the whole crew. He was a good guy, a real good guy. We miss having him around here."

"Did you ever see him act nervous or jumpy?"

"You mean was he on drugs or something? Jimmy never used. When he bought us pizza, he brought soda in with it, not beer."

"Was he ever late for work? Were there indications that he was not happy in his work?"

"Not at all. He worked hard every day; and when he was done with his workload, he usually helped one of us finish what we were doing. He cared about people. He cared about us."

Grant was getting a feeling of familiarity from Raina. She knew Jimmy more than she was saying.

"Raina, did you have a relationship with Jimmy outside of work? I mean, did you ever do things together?"

Raina studied Grant and leaned back against the car she'd been working on. Her shoulders drooped and she bowed her head.

"Yes. I did. And I only tell you this for one reason. Jimmy is a responsible man, a good man. If he new…if he…was…aware…"

Grant leaned into Raina. Her voice had softened. "If he knew what, Raina?"

"I'm pregnant," she said, unconsciously placing a hand over her stomach. "Jimmy would never have left me alone to raise our child. Something's happened to him, I know it. I'm scared and I'm worried."

Shannon's surprise was obvious, but her joy at the announcement was even *more* obvious.

"We're really sisters then," she said with a large smile on her face. "I don't care if you were married to my brother or not, you are family. You are carrying my niece or nephew and I will help you all I can. Please, let me help you."

Raina smiled at Shannon. It was the first time either Grant or Shannon had seen any emotion on her face at all, other than the pain of her disclosure. "I would like that," she said, "I would really like that."

Shannon stood up and moved to where Raina stood. She took both arms and wrapped them around her. Raina returned the hug and sobbed on Shannon's shoulders.

"It's been frighteningly lonely," she said through her tears. "Between my worry for Jimmy and wondering how I was going to handle a baby and work to support us both. But I always thought Jimmy would come back, that he'd just been on some unannounced vacation or something. But when he didn't come back after so long, when he didn't contact me, I got scared for him. I didn't know what to do."

Grant had watched the exchange and stepped into the conversation once again. "When are you off of work? It would be nice to buy you dinner and visit some more."

"I would like that," Raina said, covertly wiping the tears from her eyes. "I'm off at five."

"We'll come back and pick you up then," said Shannon, still smiling widely. She reached out and took hold of Raina's hand. "I'm so excited for you, and for Jimmy. I know if he was aware of this situation, he would be pleased and so happy. We'll find him, Raina, and bring him back to you…and to me."

Grant and Shannon hurried to their car. The arrangement was made to meet up with Sawyer and Tope and exchange information over lunch. There was a lot of information to share on their end, and they were hopeful that Sawyer and Tope had been equally successful. They drove to the diner where they were to meet the detectives, and found the two had already gotten there.

They went inside the small family diner and sat in a booth, waiting for someone to come and take their order. Eager to find out what the other had learned, they ordered their lunch and started debriefing right away.

Sawyer and Tope listened intently at Grant and Shannon's update, surprised by news of the pregnancy. Next it was the detectives' turn.

"It went pretty slowly at first," began Sawyer. "But then, everything turned around when we began knocking on doors in Jimmy's apartment complex. Two people said they saw Jimmy leaving several weeks ago with two men. It was dark, but they thought Jimmy was going willingly. At least that's what they said."

Tope took it from there. "There are a couple bits of good information from what they saw. First, Jimmy was alive three weeks ago, and they didn't kill him when they went to his apartment. That means he has information someone wanted. Or at least he did at the time. Second, it could mean that his abduction may have to do with them finding out about Shannon and making her a target, or he decided to try and leave the organization and they found out about it."

"What happens if he decides he wants to leave? What happens then?" Shannon's dark eyes were fearful, anxious.

Tope folded his hands on the table studied Shannon, wondering exactly how he would tell her the truth.

"Usually, they will go after the family, as a form of coercion, before they do anything to a trained member of the organization. That will often make the person turn around and continue, but it will also mean that he or she will be watched very carefully from that point on."

Shannon was quiet as the waitress returned with their orders. The plates of hot food were placed in front of each of them. "Can I get you anything else?"

They all let her know they were good and as she walked away, all eyes returned to Shannon.

"I'm sorry to have to tell you all that," said Tope, "but I couldn't lie to you. I felt like you needed the information straight up."

"No, no...I appreciate it," said Shannon, "I really do. But I'm putting some things together and it makes me wonder..."

"Wonder about what?" asked Grant.

"I haven't been followed since I've been back, but my apartment *was* broken into. I have no idea how that fits into any of this. I've not seen any black SUVs, no dark suits, nothing. I wondered why, but now I think it's because this organization sent that guy who followed me to Alaska and when he was killed, the SUV guys felt the threat was over. Yes?"

"Yes, the man, Hammer, was probably the one they sent to kill you." Grant picked up a fry and rolled it around between his fingers. "However, we still do not know for sure who sent those SUVs. Was it FBI? Who were they and where did they go? At the very least, we know that Jimmy is still alive. If he were dead, they would have no reason to try to harm you. And since Hammer was not successful, they will either send another killer, or threaten Jimmy with sending another one in order to keep him in line."

Tope looked doubtful. "I seriously doubt they will stop trying to get to Shannon. We need to be vigilant. Shannon could still be, and most likely is, a target."

They ate their lunches in silence, each putting the pieces of the puzzle together in their own mind. Grant barely tasted his food, almost unaware he was eating, as his thoughts turned inside his head like a giant wheel. He was sure everyone else was having the same experience.

As they finished eating, Grant spoke up. "Did you get any other information from the people you were able to talk to?"

"Not really. Many of them said much the same as Raina told you. Jimmy was a good kid that helped everyone and was a great neighbor to have. One shopkeeper told me Jimmy chased down a shoplifter for him." Sawyer popped his last fry into his mouth. "We didn't hear a single negative comment about him."

"That sounds like the Jimmy I know and love." Shannon's smile was proud, but very, very sad.

"We still have half the day," said Grant. "What do you want to do? We told Raina we would pick her up for dinner tonight. It would be good if you two would join us. You may think of questions to ask her that I did not."

"That sounds good," agreed Sawyer. "In the meantime, it would be good if we could find Jimmy's car. Did he have a car?"

"Not that I know of," replied Shannon. "He walked everywhere he went."

"We better check that out," said Grant. "Just in case. I know the furnishings in his apartment were quite a surprise for you, Shannon. We need to go have a look just to be sure."

Grant drove all four back to Jimmy's apartment complex in Shannon's SUV. Driving slowly around to the back of the complex, they found the assigned parking.

Sure enough, in the parking spot that matched Jimmy's apartment number sat a beautiful sports convertible, candy apple red with a soft top, that had been cut to shreds. The body of the car looked like it belonged to Bonnie and Clyde, covered with bullet holes shot at close range.

Grant was stunned. "No one inside mentioned this detail? How could anyone have not have heard this? When they saw it, why did no one call the police? This makes no sense."

Tope looked at Sawyer. "This explains some of why they were all so secretive. The little we did get from them was practically squeezed out. They weren't real forthcoming."

Sawyer looked up at the apartment building, taking in every inch of the structure. "When something like this happens, everyone clams up. They're all afraid of saying anything to anyone. I'd be willing to bet none of them even mentioned it to each other. They just hope the police see it and do an investigation. Nobody dares get involved."

Tope looked sideways at his partner. "You think no one said anything out of fear?"

"Fear," nodded Sawyer. "I'd be willing to bet they were threatened.

"How do you threaten a whole apartment complex?" Grant, too, was staring up at the complex.

"Maybe Jimmy made it sound like a joke, like someone had played some kind of a joke on him." Tope stared at the car.

"Maybe, but if this was my car, I sure wouldn't be laughing." Sawyer turned to Grant. "What do you think?"

"I think this car is full of bullet holes, and there is no way to tell who knew about it, who did it or if Jimmy knew of it. It could have been done to make it look like Jimmy Norton was dead, maybe after he was taken. There's no way to know for sure about any of it."

Sawyer put in a call to the local police station, telling them they needed CSI to the site immediately. While they waited, Tope peeked inside the car, looking for signs of blood. There were none, at least that he could see.

"He wasn't in the car when the shots were fired. There's no blood in there. This just smacks of Brevet. Did they say anything to you in Alaska about that crime ring?"

"Yes," said Grant. "They told us that was the name of the organization this Hammer belonged to, but nothing else."

"That's probably because they didn't know anything else," said Tope. "Nobody does. They only know the name, and that's going to make our job a lot harder."

Chapter Nineteen

The local LEOs arrived with the CSI and began their investigation of Jimmy's car. While the CSI team took over the investigation of the automobile, the officers interviewed Sawyer and Tope, especially concerning how they became aware of this car; they explained the situation.

"Why wasn't a missing persons report filed with our department?" The officer's badge said his name was Smythe.

Shannon, who'd been listening intently, stepped forward immediately. "If you will *check* your missing persons reports, you'll see a report filed by me more than two weeks ago. I was told you'd be in touch. You weren't. Your response to this call has reinforced my feeling that nothing has been done. You don't even recognize his name as an active file."

"Shannon," whispered Grant softly, "you do not want to alienate these men."

Tope pulled Officer Smythe aside and spoke with him for a few minutes. Grant wondered if he'd told them of the Brevet Organization connection, as the officer's face grew somber the more they spoke. When they were finished, Tope returned to the group and pulled them away from the crime scene, out of earshot.

"They weren't aware of the connection with organized crime. We've been given 'permission' to leave, but I gave them both your number and mine," he said, speaking to Sawyer. "I thought I'd leave you out of it, Grant, since you're here unofficially. I figured you'd have less interference in your investigation than we will." He smiled sarcastically.

The four of them left the scene and made their way back to Shannon's SUV. Sawyer and Tope needed to return to their car, and there was still the meeting for dinner with Raina.

Grant had some nagging questions about the earlier interviews at Jimmy's apartment complex. "When you spoke with the tenants in the building, there had to be people who were not home, yes?" He was thinking as he pulled the SUV out onto the main road. "Did anyone say there was another tenant, or other tenants that no one had seen in a while?"

"I can't say that the folks were happy to see us," said Sawyer. "Most wouldn't even speak to us, and those that did barely answered our questions. Now I wonder if we were asking the right questions. I never asked if there were any tenants that hadn't been seen for a while."

Shannon had been sitting quietly in the passenger seat. "I'm glad I'm not the only one who does that. The *nerve* of those men assuming no missing persons report had been filed."

Sawyer was watching Grant. "Why do you ask about the tenants who weren't home? Do you think we should go back and try to talk to them as well?"

"It is just a thought," began Grant. "I am wondering whether they were not home or were unable to answer the door."

"Unable to answer?" asked Sawyer. "Like…maybe they were dead?" Grant's eyes never left the road, but Sawyer couldn't help but think that Grant's internal compass was hard at work.

"Yes," replied Grant. "Like dead. Did anyone give you a description of the men who took Jimmy away?"

"No, it was too dark," replied Tope. "Still, why didn't someone tell us that Jimmy had a car and that it had been destroyed? That piece doesn't make sense. Someone had to hear that. And also," mused Tope, "if Jimmy was as loved as we've been hearing about from those that knew him, why didn't someone call the police if they felt Jimmy was being taken against his will?"

"It does seem the deeper we dig into this, the more questions we come away with," said Grant, now deep in thought. "But it makes sense, if these folks were threatened, they would answer questions that would not get them into trouble and nothing more."

"It's interesting," began Shannon, staring out the passenger-side window, "that we haven't seen a single black SUV since I've been back. What do you suppose that means?"

The car pulled up outside the restaurant where Sawyer had left his car. They all sat in silence for a moment.

"Hammer is dead," said Tope. "If he was the threat, once the threat was removed they were no longer needed."

"That doesn't make any sense." Sawyer's response reflected his frustration. "Wouldn't the mob just send someone else? Why not? If they had a job to do, seems to me they would keep trying until the job was done."

"Unless…" Tope's sentence trailed off before it started.

"Unless what?" Grant's eyes watched Tope in the review mirror.

Tope frowned and barely shook his head as he glanced to the front passenger seat. Grant understood exactly what he was talking about. The mob *would* keep looking unless the threat had been eliminated. Jimmy would be the threat. How would he ever explain that to Shannon?

As if on cue, Shannon suddenly came out of her thoughts. "Unless what? What are we talking about? Sorry, I was lost in memories."

"Nothing, at this point," said Grant. "We are just brainstorming."

Grant and Shannon would pick up Raina in about an hour. Sawyer decided to use the time to update Captain Amerson on the events of the day.

Sawyer and Tope got out of the car. Sawyer pulled out his phone and started for their car. Tope joined him, and Grant and Shannon waited in Shannon's SUV for the results of the conversation with the captain.

"Shannon," began Grant, "I need to talk to you. You mentioned that the people who were following you had not bothered you since you arrived back home. Did you hear that conversation in the car?"

"Not really, I was lost in thought."

"I need you to understand something." Grant wasn't sure how to proceed, but he didn't have to worry. Shannon finished the thought for him.

"Jimmy is probably dead. The only reason they would have to come after me is if Jimmy was alive and they were trying to put pressure on him."

Grant's eyebrows shot to the ceiling. "I did not think you heard that inference."

"I didn't have to hear it. I was busy thinking about that while you three were talking. I…I think I need to be realistic here, and I'm not sure how to do that. I *try* to imagine he's gone, but my mind just won't let me believe it."

"There could be other reasons they called off the hit on you, Shannon. Jimmy may have agreed to whatever they were telling him had to be done. He could have been told that you were a target and would be eliminated unless he did whatever it was they were asking of him. It does not necessarily mean he is dead."

"You really think so?"

"Yes, I do."

Shannon's head fell to her chest and a huge sigh escaped her. She shook her head. "He has a child on the way, a great job that he loved, a woman who loved him, and then there's *me*. He had *me*. There is so much that he has to live for, why would he get himself involved with people like these? I've tried so hard to understand what he was thinking, but I just can't wrap my head around it."

"Sometimes the web is wrapped around them so gradually that they cannot see what is happening until it has happened. Much like the spider and the fly. By the time Jimmy was aware of who these people really were, it was too late."

"I often think that it might be better if he were dead. If he's done awful things for these people, it might be the easier thing. Then he wouldn't have to live with the regret his actions would cause him."

"There is always a way back. The trick is finding him so we can help him find it. You are correct, Shannon, he has much to live for. It could be that he does not realize it."

Grant thought for a moment. "Shannon, have you ever shot a gun?"

"No, I haven't. Jimmy was really enjoying the shooting range and tried to get me to go with him for a while, but I really wasn't interested.

"I have never been particularly interested in guns, either, but my grandfather insisted I learn to shoot, which I did." Grant smiled at the memory. "I found I had a strong dislike for guns, but I did learn a life lesson from it all. Did Jimmy ever talk to you about the recoil of a gun?"

"I think he might have mentioned it. I know I've heard of it."

"Depending on the gun, and if it is held correctly, the recoil can be very mild, or it can do some damage. It is also referred to as 'kick back' and the bigger the gun, the harder the recoil. The force of the bullet leaving the chamber causes the gun to push back or 'kick back' against the shoulder or the hand. On larger caliber guns, such as those used by the military, the recoil can be deadly. My grandfather compared it to life, and how the bigger the mess we make for ourselves, the bigger the recoil will be in our lives. In some cases, the consequences of our choices can be deadly."

"Your grandfather sounds like a very wise man. I wish I could have known him."

"He would have liked you very much."

Shannon turned to him. There was a heavy sadness that Grant wished he could take from her. "You have strong roots to your family," she said softly. "I loved my mother and father, and I remember my grandfather, but not very much. He died when I was small, so I never got to know him. My parents' siblings left when I was very young and I never knew any of them. I guess we weren't your typical native family."

"There are few 'typical' native families left. But you must remember, whether they are near or far, they are still your family. You can still honor them by the life you live. I think you do that very well. Your parents would be proud of how you have worked to find Jimmy."

"Maybe. I'm kind of glad I'll be returning to work on Monday. I think I need a break from all of this. If you fill me in each evening, that will be good enough for me."

"I can do that. I hear the fatigue in your voice. It might be good for you to have a rest from this."

Sawyer returned to Shannon's car. Grant rolled down the window as he approached.

"Captain says to keep up the good work. He didn't have any information for us from his end, but I didn't expect that he would. We'll head over to the restaurant and wait for you there."

"Thank you, Sawyer. We will meet you there." Sawyer returned to his car and Grant rolled the window back up and headed to the auto shop.

Grant and Shannon arrived at the shop to pick up Raina and found a very different woman waiting for them. Tall, slender, dressed in clean jeans and a white blouse, tucked in at the waist. With a sparkle in her blue eyes they'd not seen previously, Raina's blond hair was washed and piled high on her head. All signs of grease and grime were gone.

Shannon squeaked and jumped from the car, hurrying around the front to greet Raina with a huge hug. "You look absolutely stunning! I'm so happy to get to see you again. Hop in and we'll be off."

Raina was equally as happy to see Shannon. She slid into the back seat as Shannon returned to the passenger's side of the car. Grant had remained in the car during the greeting, giving the two women more opportunity to bond. It was obvious to him that Raina was very good for Shannon's heart at this difficult time in her life.

As Raina shut the door she chuckled. "I thought I would wear my blouse tucked in while I still could."

"How are you feeling?" asked Shannon.

"I'm better each day," Raina replied. "It's nice to be able to work through the day and not have to run to the bathroom every hour to throw up."

The two women chatted and laughed together as Grant drove to the restaurant. He watched the exchange, quietly observing Raina without being too obvious. She seemed genuine and honest in her interactions with Shannon. She was no longer hiding anything and her conversation made that obvious. It was good to see Shannon smiling. She hadn't done much of that of late.

The three of them met up with Sawyer and Tope at the restaurant and went inside where they were seated at a table. As the conversation began to lag, Raina stared at her hands resting in her lap.

"Are you okay, Raina? Are you feeling sick again?" Shannon touched her arm softly.

"No, no I'm fine. It's just that I probably wasn't completely honest with you when we talked at the shop. There *is* more I can tell you about Jimmy, but I wanted to make sure you were who you said you were first. I can see that you love Jimmy very much and that you have a great support group in these men."

Shannon nodded. She looked around the table with thankful pride. "Yes, I do. They are good friends."

Raina continued, "There are some things you need to know, some things Jimmy told me that might help you find him. We worked very hard to keep our relationship a secret from the shop, because we didn't know how the owner would react. But Jimmy got even more secretive as time went on, and he went to great lengths to make sure we were seen by *no one* when we met after work. Those meetings got fewer and further between, until the morning I came into work and was going to tell him about the baby. He refused to talk to me, to be seen with me."

"That must have hurt you a great deal," said Grant.

"It…it did, but more than hurt me, it scared me. Jimmy sometimes got a look in his eyes that…that was…it was…frightening. I started to avoid him as much as he did me. It was almost like he was working very hard to be mean and threatening."

"One day, just before he stopped coming to work, he got that evil look in his eyes and told me if I ever came near him again…" Raina's eyes filled with Tears. "If…if I ever came near him again, he…he would kill me."

Chapter Twenty

Shannon gasped and both hands flew to her mouth. Her dark, charcoal eyes were fixed on Raina. "He said that to you? He said those exact words?"

"I'll never forget it as long as I live. Those were *his* words." Raina was blinking back tears, refusing to let them fall. "At first I thought it was because of the baby, that he didn't want a baby. But then I knew he couldn't know I was pregnant because I hadn't even told my mother. *No one* knew about the baby yet. There was nothing else I could think, but that he didn't want *me*. He turned and left work right after he said it and didn't return. I never saw him again."

Using her napkin, Raina dabbed at the tears that threatened to fall. Shannon reached over and touched her arm. "There are other issues at play here Raina. I can guarantee that he was saying that to protect you. He didn't want the people he'd gotten involved with to find you. He didn't want them to know about you. Somehow, they found out about me, and they tried to kill me. I know my brother. He would never be so cruel unless there was a good reason."

Grant picked up his menu. "I think we need to give this conversation a chance to sink in." He glanced at Sawyer. "What are you having?"

All eyes at the table turned to Grant. The sensitive one, the gentle, old soul was ordering dinner in spite of what had just been revealed? Could it be true?

"What are you all staring at? I just said the women at the table needed some time to think. It only makes sense if we just breathe and stop gawking at them, they will then be allowed to process what has been said."

"Gawking?" Sawyer's mouth was practically hanging open. "Did you say, *gawking*?"

"I did," replied Grant, quietly perusing his menu, "and I meant it."

If the conversation hadn't been so emotional, Tope and Sawyer would have been laughing. As it was, all Sawyer could think to say was, "I didn't think you used that kind of language."

"Gawking is not a curse. It is simply a verb, an action word, it denotes-"

"I'm fine," said Raina, breaking into the conversation. "Really. It was a while ago."

"Just so you know," said Shannon, with a wise nod, "when I get my hands on that boy he's going to be sorry for the day our father first kissed our mother. Okay, I'll hug him first and give him a kiss on the forehead, *then* I'll make him sorry."

Raina burst out laughing and the tension was released. "You guys are hilarious!" she said, gazing fondly at her dinner companions. "Kind of like…who were those comedian guys?" She looked questioningly at Shannon.

"The Three Stooges," replied Shannon, flatly.

"Yeah, those guys," said Raina as she picked up her menu and began browsing. "There would be four, though, if I counted you." She smirked as she glanced at Shannon.

Shannon returned the smirk and shot a disgusted look at the three men who immediately began defending their actions.

Sawyer jumped right in. "We were only saying that Grant doesn't usually use words like 'gawking' when he speaks."

"I wasn't even saying anything," said Tope. "I was just listening."

Shannon shook her head and turned to her menu. "Pathetic. All of you." Then she turned to Raina. "Are you okay?"

Raina smiled. "I am. I feel better having told you all that. I really do."

Grant was still reading the menu, but laid it down. "Now, see? I was right. They just need some time to process the information."

Tope shook his head and muttered under his breath, "I'm totally innocent of all charges." Sawyer just shook his head and Shannon and Raina chuckled softly.

Once their food was ordered, Raina asked, "What people are you talking about? You mentioned Jimmy was involved with what sounded to me like some bad people."

"That is a conversation for another time," said Sawyer, "In the meantime, no more talking shop. We are going to have a good meal and spend some time getting to know our new friend. Welcome, Raina, to the group I like to refer to as 'the crazies.' "

They enjoyed both their meal together and getting to know more about Raina and how she came to work as an auto repair technician. She apparently had an older brother whom she adored and the only way she ever got to spend any time with him was under a car, where she learned how to fix *anything* when it came to cars. And she enjoyed it. So it was that, pretty much her whole life, she'd worked repairing automobiles.

"You will be a nice addition to our family," said Shannon, smiling. "And I'm looking forward to helping you out with my little niece or nephew."

"I look forward to that as well."

Once dinner was finished, Grant and Shannon took Raina to the shop where she'd left her car.

"Thank you for a fun night," she said as she opened her door. "I had a great time."

"We did, too." Shannon got out of the car and gave Raina a hug. "I hope you don't mind. I'm a real hugger."

"I absolutely don't mind! I haven't had a hug for several months now. I miss them."

She turned and walked around the back of the car. Shannon watched to make sure she got safely to her car and then slid back into her seat, closing the door.

"You speak of us like an old married couple when you say that *we* had a good time," teased Grant.

"I guess I did. I must be getting used to you." Shannon smiled that sly smile she would get every now and then.

"Like an old shoe?"

"Like a *favorite* old shoe. You know, well worn, worth every penny you spent on it and you're worried it will wear out and you'll never find another one like it."

Grant laughed at her description. "I might wear out as time goes on, but you will never have to look for another one."

Shannon grinned and settled into her seat. It had been a good night, and Grant was thankful to see her happy.

Once Sawyer and Tope were on their way back to Blakely, Shannon and Grant headed to her apartment.

"I like her." Shannon had her head back against the headrest and turned to gaze at Grant.

"She seems like a very nice person," agreed Grant. "You two act like you have known each other for much longer than a few days."

"I can sure see why she was so mistrusting of me the first time I went into the shop. I wonder if she thought all my family was rude and verbally abusive. She certainly didn't need to be spoken to like that. Jimmy could have at least found a better way to say it."

"When our words are spoken in fear, they often come out wrong. The heart is always right, but not everyone takes the time to consider that. Words are awfully powerful."

They pulled up in front of Shannon's apartment complex. She glanced up at her window and noticed a light was on in her living room. Grant noticed as well, but Shannon gasped and whispered, "Jimmy."

She took off at a run with Grant behind her trying to get her to stop.

"Shannon, wait. Shannon! You have to wait. You do not know who is up there, if anyone. Shannon!"

There was no stopping her. She took the stairs two at a time and raced down the hallway. Grant was right behind her; afraid to grab her arm for fear he would be dragged along behind as she continued toward her apartment door. As she was just about to reach the door she started to call out Jimmy's name again.

Grant was finally able to take her arm and move her as gently as he could against the hallway wall. He quickly placed his hand over her mouth and whispered to her. "Shannon, think, think what you have been through these past weeks. What if it is not Jimmy in there? What if it is a trap?"

Both of them were breathing heavily and Grant removed his hand from over her mouth.

"What if it *is* Jimmy? He's waiting for me! I have to get in there."

"If it is Jimmy, he is not going anywhere. The door has not opened. Please, allow me to go in first." Grant waited for a couple of seconds for his words to sink in. "Will you do that?"

Shannon gave her head a single nod and stared down the hallway to her apartment door. "Okay," she said, still out of breath.

Grant walked slowly to the door and gingerly turned the knob. It wasn't locked. "Did you lock this door when we left?" he whispered to her. Shannon had followed him and was standing behind him now.

"Yes, I always do," she whispered back.

"Did Jimmy have a key?"

"Yes."

Grant motioned for her to wait before going in. He opened the door carefully, looking for any wires or traps. There were none. As the door opened more, he saw a man in a nicely dressed suit sitting comfortably in one of Shannon's easy chairs. Grant turned to Shannon, watching her reaction to the voice. This man was not Jimmy. How would she respond? He reached for her hand and guided her through the doorway.

"Please, please, come in." The man's voice was mild and pleasant.

"I'm afraid I don't understand why I would need an invitation to enter my own apartment." Shannon was angry and her venom-filled words flew from her mouth. She moved past Grant instead of waiting, releasing his hand and crossed her arms.

"I'm sorry to have to come in uninvited, but I thought if I was sitting in the dark it would be more unnerving than if you expected someone to be here when you saw the light on."

"You could have waited until I got home," she said, her eyes raging with fire. "Most *civil* people would, anyway. What do you want?"

Grant was aware of every cell in his body. He could feel the hairs on the back of his neck standing to attention, aware that his muscles were tightening, his jaw set.

"I couldn't risk being seen, and I needed to speak with you." The man held up both hands so Grant could see he wasn't armed. "Please, sit down. You will be interested in what I have to say."

Grant had taken Shannon's arm to hold her back. He led her to the couch, afraid if he let go, she would jump this guy and put him in a headlock before he had time to know what hit him.

"I asked you what you wanted. *What do you want?*" Shannon's voice had a very sharp edge to it. It was clear she was angry…and determined.

The man sighed and reached into the front of his suit coat. "I'm only getting my credentials. I'm not armed. I'm not here to hurt you."

He pulled out a small black leather wallet and opened it up for them to see. "I'm with the FBI and was instructed to come and speak with you about your brother. My name is Trevyn James."

Shannon tensed. "Jimmy? Where is he? Is he safe?"

"We don't know," said Trevyn, "but we are working at finding out, and we need you to stop your investigation."

"Why?" Shannon's voice was demanding, strong. "We found his car full of bullet holes. Did you know about that? Apparently, you're not doing much to 'find out' about my brother."

"We are aware of the car, but we had to leave it where it was, untouched. We don't want the Brevet to know we're aware of anything having to do with Jimmy. You hanging around this apartment complex and calling in the cops about the car is endangering our investigation. If the Brevet thought Jimmy wasn't missed by anyone, they sure know that he is now. And that could place anyone close to Jimmy in jeopardy."

"We could help you, if you would like," Grant's calm had returned. "I have some experience with law enforcement."

"And you are…?"

"My name is Grant Mulvane."

"I've heard of you. You've made quite a name for yourself, at least in Iowa."

"A good name, I hope." Grant's eyes never left Trevyn's face.

"Yes, all good. However, I would have to ask my superiors about your helping out."

Shannon was anxious for the subject to return to Jimmy. "You said we would be interested in what you have to say."

Trevyn's eyes settled on Shannon. "We need you to know that Jimmy was one of the good guys. He worked with us for about a year, prior to his disappearance."

"We already know that."

"Yes, I know you do. Several months ago, Jimmy's contact with his handler became sporadic. We knew something was up, but we weren't sure what. Within a few weeks of missed appointments, Jimmy had disappeared. We think he was taken in by the Brevet organization. We've been trying to extract him, but we can't find him."

Grant shook his head, forcing himself to breathe. "Why would you put an inexperienced young man on a job with an organization like the Brevet? He had no idea what he was getting into." Grant was working to keep his voice level, his anger at bay.

"The organization actually contacted him. A man named Hammer befriended Jimmy at the shooting range."

Grant cleared his throat. "That man, Hammer, tried to kill Shannon when she was at my home in Alaska. He is dead."

"Yes, I know. We killed him."

Chapter Twenty-One

Grant studied Trevyn, weighing his words heavily before speaking. "There were no shots fired *at* my house. The only shot fired was the one that killed Hammer. What happened?"

Trevyn sighed heavily and began, "We sent in a team of FBI agents to keep an eye on Hammer. The reports that they made to us were that he had been nonviolent, appearing to observe only. However, it was especially dark that night and it looked like he'd pulled a gun from his coat." Trevyn paused, a look of guilty disappointment shown on his face. "When they went to inspect the body, they found he'd only taken out a pair of binoculars. It was our error."

Shannon pulled her hair back, running her fingers over the top of her head, a nervous habit that Grant had seen often of late. "So, what does all that mean for Jimmy?"

"That's just the problem. We don't know what it means. We only know that Jimmy was "escorted" from his apartment by two men and hasn't been seen since."

"Why didn't the Brevet just send someone else?" asked Grant. "Not that I'd want anyone else to threaten Shannon, but it just seems like they would've considered Hammer a necessary expenditure and sent someone else to kill her."

"We don't know. No one knows anything about the Brevet, no one had even *seen* a member of the organization until Hammer was found. The only way they knew it was him was that we got lucky a couple of years ago, and managed to get a sample of his DNA. When we compared it to the dead man at your place, we knew we had the right guy."

Grant could almost hear Shannon's wheels turning. "So, you don't know where Jimmy is, you don't know what this man's death has to do with Jimmy, and you don't know who took him…just what *do* you know?"

"We know Jimmy is missing. We know he was working with us and then he wasn't. We know he's a good guy, and that if he's now in the Brevet organization, he's probably not the brother you remember. Those things we're fairly clear on. The rest is a guessing game."

"Well, then, can you at least tell me who was following me prior to my leaving for Alaska? Surely you know *that* much."

Trevyn studied Shannon for a moment. "That was the FBI trying to decide if you were part of Jimmy's disappearance."

"*WHAT?*" Grant could feel Shannon's shock so strongly he was amazed Trevyn couldn't feel it. "You thought I would be part of Jimmy's disappearance? What's the matter with you people? Are you all crazy?"

Trevyn smiled softly. "I wonder that myself, sometimes. But, no, we're not all crazy. You have to understand, Shannon, that we didn't know you. These things happen more than you or I care to think about. We had to be sure. When we realized the Brevet was after you, we were certain you had nothing to do with Jimmy's disappearance. You have to know we were just following up on a lead, which is standard procedure."

The room fell quiet and Grant was the next to speak. "Shannon, you said you were going back to work on Monday. That is going to be the safest place for you. I will drop you off and pick you up each day. It is the only way I will know you are safe. Are you agreeable to that?"

"I guess I'll have to be," she said with a shrug. "If it will help for me to be out of your hair, then I need to do it."

"I only need you to be safe, nothing else." Grant knew there was something else, but his feelings for her only underlined the need for her to be safe.

A look of concern briefly swept Trevyn's face. "She may not be as safe as you think she would be. We may have to send in some undercover agents to guarantee that safety."

Shannon's shocked "NO way," was covered by Grants relieved "Good idea." Shannon gaped at Grant.

Taking her hand, Grant spoke softly, reassuring her. "You must not be left without some protection, Shannon. We cannot think the organization will leave you alone until we have Jimmy back. They may yet try to use you for leverage with him. It would be irresponsible to leave you at the office with no cover."

"He's correct, Shannon. You will need protection. It's much better to over protect than it is to wish we'd done something after the fact." Trevyn's attention turned to Grant. "Are you willing to work with me, Grant, assuming it is approved by my superiors?" Trevyn sat back in the easy chair and waited for an answer.

"I am. I will need to let Sawyer and Tope know they are no longer needed."

"That has already been done. They are aware, and they most emphatically informed me that you would not step aside. They also said you would be a great asset to the investigation and that we should make sure you stay on board. They have great respect for you."

"And I for them."

Trevyn stood and moved to the door. He stopped with his hand on the knob. Turning back to Grant he handed him a card from the inside pocket of his coat. "Please call me when you have dropped Shannon at work on Monday. You will leave her car at her work and I will pick you up at the diner just south of her office building."

"What do we do until then?" Shannon rose from the couch and waited for an answer.

"You will do nothing. Stay out of sight, away from your windows, either at work or here. Do nothing."

With that, he was out the door, his footsteps fading down the hall.

Shannon plopped down on the couch, exhausted and afraid, both emotions keeping her anger at bay. "He expects us to sit around here and do nothing?"

"Yes, he does, and so do I. The FBI has far more resources than even Sawyer and Tope have." Grant joined Shannon on the couch. "I will call and talk with the two of them, and I will keep them apprised of the investigation, at least as much as I am allowed ."

Shannon started to protest and Grant broke in, "Yes, and you as well, of course. It would be difficult to not speak of the investigation if I am staying here at night." He smiled softly. "You will know first, then I will share with Sawyer and Tope."

Her arms went around his neck and she laid her head on his shoulder. "The smartest thing I ever did was go to Alaska and get you."

"I would have to agree," chuckled Grant. He pulled Shannon closer to him.

Shannon lifted her head. Keeping her arms around his neck she gaped at him in mock surprise. "And here I've been thinking how humble you are."

Grant released her and stood. He stepped to the window. "I should not tease like that. I apologize." He stared into the darkness of the night.

"I was just kidding, you know, because I knew *you* were kidding," said Shannon. She stood and followed Grant. "Did I make you uncomfortable just then?"

Grant turned to face her. "You consistently make me uncomfortable, Shannon Norton. Consistently."

"I…I'm sorry. I don't mean to do that." She softly touched his arm.

"It is not a bad thing, Shannon," replied Grant, covering her hand with his. "I often wonder what I will do when I return to Alaska and enter my home. It has always been a comfort to me, a place of refuge. Now, you will not be there, and suddenly I feel loneliness when I think of home."

"I will miss you, too."

Grant moved to reach the curtain rod and slowly closed the curtains as he spoke. "I have never experienced the type of feelings you awaken in me. It is difficult for me to explain them, even to myself, let alone to you. It is as if I have waited all my life for you to come to me. When I saw you in my barn that night, I knew who you were. I had not been able to get you out of my mind since I first saw you that day in your office with Sawyer. Now I fear if our lips meet, I will lose myself in this feeling."

"I believe that only happens when the feeling is one-sided. It isn't, Grant."

"The Spirits have told me this, but I did not feel now was the time to tell you how I felt. We must put these feelings aside until Jimmy is found. I cannot ask for your heart when I know it is consumed with finding your brother."

Grant finished with the curtains and stared at them, as if hoping for answers to questions he wasn't he sure he knew to ask.

Shannon moved in behind Grant. She put her arms around his waist and held him. "Grant, once I commit myself to you, there will be no one else who will ever consume my heart. Only you. I have never known such respect from a man, and such selflessness."

"And I have never known anyone with such a beautiful spirit as you possess. I have searched for you, saved myself for you, all my life." Grant turned in Shannon's arms to return the embrace. With her head against his chest, he spoke softly into her beautiful, black hair. "We will find Jimmy, bring him home and then we will see where our hearts lead us."

§§§

Jimmy lay on the cold cement floor of the warehouse. His ribs ached, his eyes were nearly swollen shut and he thought maybe his arm was broken. Pain was everywhere.

Days before, and he wasn't even sure how many at this point, two men from the organization had hauled him from his apartment and into a waiting van. He was tossed on the floor of the van behind the driver's seat, and while the driver sped off, Jimmy's head was covered with a cloth bag and his hands and feet tied.

They'd found out about his attempt to leave the organization. He'd been so careful, keeping every detail of his escape to himself, even changing his name. How could they have found out?

However they found out, the deed was known, and Jimmy had paid the price. He had no idea why he was still alive, but now he prayed to the Spirits to allow him to live just long enough to see his sister one last time. He was willing to pay for the crimes he'd committed, but he had to say goodbye to Shannon.

The warehouse floor was icy cold and his body was trembling. He wondered if he was going into shock.

"This is just a shame, Jimmy. A real shame." The voice of his boss came through the darkness.

"Jayce? Is that you?" Jimmy could barely recognize his own voice. His face must be more swollen than he realized.

Jimmy felt someone kneel down beside him. "Get me a mattress and a blanket," Jayce called to the darkness. He returned to Jimmy. "I never wanted this to happen, Jimmy. What were you thinking? You know once you're part of this family, you are part of the family forever."

"I...I know," began Jimmy, trying to ignore the pain. "I just wanted to see my sister. I wouldn't have told her anything...you know I wouldn't. I wasn't leaving the family, I was only going to say hello."

"Your sister is dead. Hammer killed her, and then the FBI killed him. At least we think that's what happened. Either way, Shannon is dead, and I'm sorry Jimmy. I'm sorry it had to be that way."

Jimmy felt like Jayce had ripped his heart out with his bare hands. Tears of fury and frustration came, but they could barely make their way out of his swollen eyes. He cried out in pain as he was lifted onto the mattress and covered with a heavy blanket. He barely noticed the smell of sweat and urine emanating from the mattress, barely noticed the softness was warmer than the floor. A chill grew in the center of his heart and was growing outward, consuming him.

"*WHY?* She meant nothing to you! She would never have harmed any of you. Why did you have to kill her?"

Jayce was shorter than Jimmy, with dark eyes and thick curly brown hair. He'd always shown great trust in Jimmy, always been kind and helpful. How could he have become a monster overnight? Which lead the young killer to the thought that just possibly Jayce may have always been a monster. How much more had he missed by focusing only on the seduction of the money they gave him?

Jayce left him in the warehouse with daylight peeking softly through the small windows along the top of the walls. What was the point of giving him a blanket and a filthy mattress? Was that expected to soften the blow of learning that Shannon was dead?

Shannon…I'm so sorry. I took your life from you because of the choices I made. I didn't know! I didn't know they would come after you. Please forgive me.

His tears fell, and the sobs were uncontrollable. With the very last part of him that the ice had not taken, and no thought of who heard him, he screamed into the empty air, "NOOO! Not Shannon! You've taken every bit of humanity I had left in me. Not Shannon!"

§§§

In the darkness of the still shadowed corner, Jayce smiled with satisfaction. He turned to the man set with the task of guarding the prisoner. "That's what I needed to hear. Show him kindness now. Show him that we are his family; that this was just a lesson to be learned. Give him a couple days to think about things, then get a doctor in here and get him cleaned up. We have lots more work for him to do."

Heading for the door, Jayce turned back to his employee. Speaking softly so not to be overheard he said, "Oh, and find Shannon Norton and get rid of her."

"Yes, sir."

Chapter Twenty-Two

Monday morning came, and Grant drove Shannon to work. Trevyn had set up two female agents as office staff to work undercover as bodyguards. They'd been given specific instructions that she was not to leave their line of sight at any time. Both Grant and Shannon had been informed of the agents' presence, along with the director of Shannon's department, but they were the only ones who were aware of the situation.

Grant escorted Shannon to her office and once she was settled in, he walked the two blocks to the diner, per Trevyn James' instructions. When Grant arrived at the diner, Trevyn was already there and seated in a booth, waiting for him. Grant motioned to him that he had a call to make and Trevyn nodded. Grant stepped outside at make his call.

"Kingsley."

"Hey, Cousin. I just wanted to say how sorry I am for the way this all came down. Do you or Tope have any idea who this Trevyn James is?"

"Tope has heard of him. Said he works in some special ops type of unit within the FBI, but doesn't know anything other than that."

"Well, I am not happy with how this is turning out."

"Don't worry about us, Grant. We just want Shannon to find her brother. Just don't plan on flying back to Alaska without spending some time with me. You got that?"

Grant smiled. "Got it. I will keep in touch."

"You do that. I'll be here."

The call ended and Grant made his way down the aisle of the diner to where Trevyn was seated. He'd ordered Grant's breakfast along with his own and it had just been delivered to the table.

"This looks good," smiled Grant. "Thank you."

"You're welcome," replied Trevyn. "My mother always said no one should start a day without a good breakfast."

"Mothers are like that, I believe." Grant picked up his cup and took a careful sip of the hot liquid. He could see Trevyn was staring at him. "Can I help you with something?"

Trevyn's laugh displayed a certain amount of discomfort. "Is it true you can find ghost prints in a snowstorm?"

Grant let go with a laugh that came up from his belly. "Now *that* is one I have not heard before. I have never actually tried that particular challenge, therefore, I could not tell you if I could do it." Grant laughed again. "Quite original, that one."

"You are a legend. We all heard about how you helped Sawyer Kingsley find the serial killer when you worked with him. You're certainly unique in your approach to tracking. Where did you learn how to do that?"

"It was not actually learned," began Grant. "My grandfather said I was born with it. It is something I have always known how to do. I believe it comes from my ancestors, and I thank them for it every day."

"You are Native Alaskan?"

"Yes, I am."

"You do them proud, Grant. It's an amazing gift you possess, and you use it well."

"Thank you for that. Now, do we have a plan for finding Jimmy Norton? What do you know that we did not discover?"

"We have mostly followed up on what you and your friends found. I'm afraid you got further on this than we did, a rare occurrence. We do know that the man, Hammer, was searching for an addition to the family when he found Jimmy. We are also aware that this organization owns at least two warehouses in the city, possibly three. That was not an easy thing to uncover. I only just found out about it this morning."

"Could they be holding Jimmy in one of these warehouses?"

"It's certainly a possibility. It's going to be tough getting inside. If they are keeping him at one of those, they will have eyes all over the place. It will take a few days to determine if there is one of these buildings that has some unusual activity."

"Jimmy may not have a few days, Trevyn. If we are to find him, we need to move now."

"Yes, I understand that. However, we have been able to learn that when Jimmy was taken, there was a ripple in the organization. This 'ripple' may be enough to disrupt their plans and give us some time to get in, grab Jimmy, and get out again."

"How do you know of this ripple?"

"I'm not at liberty to say."

"Well, then, what was the ripple?"

"Again, it's not something I can talk about."

Grant rose and laid his napkin on the table. "I will call Sawyer and Tope. We will find Jimmy, as we had planned. It is useless working with hands tied behind my back, and I will not even attempt it. If you cannot treat me as an equal, I will not work with you." He started for the door when Trevyn called out to him.

"Grant, wait."

Grant stopped and turned around to face Trevyn, who was still seated in the booth.

"Come back, let's talk about this."

"I have nothing further to say on the subject. I believe I was fairly clear on my points."

"Grant, please. Sit down."

Against his better judgment, Grant returned to the booth and slipped into his seat. "If you will not answer my questions, I see no need to continue this partnership. It was not my idea in the first place."

"I understand. Let me explain. We know there was a ripple in the organization because we have another informant who replaced Jimmy."

"And what did he tell you?"

"The informant is female."

Grant could feel a hole forming in the pit of his stomach. The next question he asked was one he would rather not know the answer to, and yet his need pushed him to ask it. "Her name is Raina, is it not?"

Trevyn sat back hard in the seat, his hands dropped to his side. "How could you possibly know that?"

"Do you know that she is pregnant? Did she tell you that?"

"She told *you*? Why would she tell you and not us?"

Grant sighed. This was not good news and his heart ached for Shannon. How would he tell her this? How would he explain why the FBI would do this to her twice? "I have no idea what her motivations are, but you must pull her from this assignment immediately. It is not safe for her or her baby."

"Who is the father, did she tell you that?"

Grant looked dumbfounded. "Did she not tell you she had a relationship with Jimmy Norton?"

Now it was Trevyn's turn. His frustration was obvious. "No, she did not. We were aware she worked at the same auto shop as he did, but we saw nothing that would make us think they were a couple."

"That is as Jimmy wanted it to be. He worked very hard to keep their relationship a secret. I am sure he was afraid of what would happen if the organization found out about them. I suggest we go to the shop and check on her. You can let her know her informant days are over." Grant stood to go.

"Now wait just a minute," Trevyn's voice was firm, demanding. "She's doing a great job for us, and we'd lose a good line of information if we just cut her off like that. It might be dangerous for her as well."

"I cannot believe you are, in the least, interested in her wellbeing. Do not try to stick that in as an afterthought to the conversation. She is in grave danger, and the *only* reason she is doing this for you is that she is hopeful it will lead her to Jimmy. You may have just dug a grave not only for her, but for her baby as well. I will go back to the office and use the SUV I parked there, or you can give me a ride. Either way, I am going to the shop to check on Raina." Grant turned and headed for the door.

Before his feet hit the sidewalk, he could feel Trevyn behind him. Trevyn called out to Grant, "Wait. We'll take my car. We need to make sure they aren't watching her work before we go in there. I'll drive."

"Whatever you feel is necessary. You will drive quickly, or I will drive, even if I have to leave you behind."

Trevyn knew, from the determined look on Grant's face, that he meant what he said. They ran to the car, parked only a block away. Try as he might, Grant couldn't erase the feeling that was creeping into the pit of his stomach. This would change everything. *Everything.*

His mind went right to the Spirits, to the spirit of his father and grandfather. *Keep her safe for Shannon. And keep the new life safe inside her. I ask you not to allow Shannon to have to deal with another loss. I am not sure she could take it. Help me, Father. Help me, Grandfather. I cannot do this without you.*

As the car approached the street where the shop was located, Trevyn pulled to the curb and parked the car among others also parked there. "We'll walk the rest of the way. If there *are* eyes on the shop, it could get sticky from here. Stay behind me."

Grant did as he was asked and as they came to the corner, Trevyn peeked slowly around the building. He pulled back and leaned against the building. "I don't see anyone, but it's hard to know if they are watching from other buildings. Let's take the alley. We'll come in the back of the garage."

They backtracked the way they'd come and found the alley halfway down the block. It was narrow, and the buildings around it had no windows on the side facing the alley.

Trevyn tried the back door leading into the shop. It wasn't locked. He opened the door slowly and peered into the shop. There were several technicians working on cars and trucks. All appeared as it should be. He entered and went into the office of the manager.

"How can I help you?" The manager was friendly, his nametag said Sam, and he stood as the men entered. His greasy belly hung out from under the tightly buttoned uniform shirt of the business. His smile was large and held no malice. Trevyn held out his hand to shake Sam's. "You don't want to shake these hands. It'll take you days to get the grease off you." He chuckled.

"We're looking for Raina. Is she about?" Trevyn lowered his hand to his side.

"No, she hasn't shown herself or answered her phone for two days now. That isn't like her. We're all pretty worried."

He was uncomfortable, he knew something he wasn't saying, or maybe he was hiding something. Grant wasn't sure which it was, but it took every ounce of self-control he had to keep from grabbing the man and forcing the information out of him. So unlike himself, and he knew it, but this was the family of the woman he cared very much about. He'd never been in this position before. But he was certainly there now. Somehow, Grant remained calm and spoke with an even, soft voice. "You know where she is."

Sam chuckled and his large belly wiggled. "I wish. She-"

"You *know* something about this situation." Grant's voice was louder this time, and more direct. "You will tell us...*now*."

"Who are you? Are you not hearing what I'm telling you? Raina hasn't shown up for work for two days. She's not answering her phone. If I knew where she was don't you think I'd be all over that? She's one of my best employees."

Trevyn stepped in, shooting Grant a warning glance. "Did she say anything before she left work? Did she have any visitors?"

Grant touched Trevyn's arm. "Speak with me, privately." He nodded to the door of the office.

"Give us a minute, Sam, would you?" Trevyn tipped his head questioningly at Sam.

"Sure." Sam's, his eyes darted from Trevyn to Grant and back to Trevyn, calculating and elusive. Fortunately, Grant knew there was only one way out of this office, and they were about to close that door. Trevyn and Grant went into the back of the shop area, closing the door behind them. Standing in front of the closed door, Trevyn remembered who he had helping him on this investigation, a piece of information he'd temporarily forgotten.

"You know something?"

"I know that *he* knows something," said Grant, nodding in the direction of the manager who was on the other side of the office door. "He knows a lot more than he is saying, and I believe he is the key to this whole situation. He is not as big a low-life as he would have you believe."

"And just how do you know this?"

Grant tipped his head to one side, just slightly, and tossed a look of "*really*....?" toward Trevyn. There was no time for him to explain where these feelings came from. He knew his attitude was slipping, that his attitude was bordering on prideful, but it couldn't be helped. He would do what he must to help Shannon and Raina, and hopefully Jimmy, and he would meditate later.

"Oh, yes, right," said Trevyn as he gazed back through the window into the manager's office. "You're Grant Mulvane. Right."

"I cannot tell you how I know, I can only tell you that this man knows far more than he is saying."

Trevyn opened the door and returned to the desk of the manager. Sam was sweating lightly by now; his eyes stayed on the papers that littered his desk. "Sam, my name is Trevyn James and this is my associate, Grant Mulvane." He pulled his credentials from the pocket of his jacket and flashed them at Sam. "I am with the FBI and Grant, here, is consulting on a case we're working on. I'm going to need you to come with me. We just want to ask you a few more questions."

That was about all it took. Sam glanced toward the door and with his full weight behind him, started out at a dead run. Unfortunately for Sam, Grant stood between him and the exit. Using the force of his body and the forward motion of Sam's, Grant grabbed the man as he attempted to get to the door. He took Sam's arm and with a quick twist and lift, Sam spun in the air and came down hard on his back. All work in the shop ceased. This convinced Trevyn that Grant was correct. There was more to this man than he'd originally seen.

The workers ran toward the manager's office and Trevyn tossed some cuffs to Grant. "Put these on him while I put out this fire."

Grant could hear Trevyn call to the workers as they approached him. "There is nothing to worry about." He held out his credentials again, so they could see them. "My name is Trevyn James. I'm with the FBI and I just want to ask your boss a few more questions. We'll return him to you shortly. We're not going to hurt him. Please step back and let us through."

Trevyn and Grant led Sam from the shop and into Trevyn's car. They proceeded to the FBI field office. Leading him down the hallway to the interrogation rooms, they opened the door and Trevyn motioned for Sam to have a seat at the small table in the center of the room. Trevyn checked the cuffs to make sure they were secure and Trevyn and Grant left the room, locking the door behind them.

The two men proceeded to the observation room and stood in front of the large one-way window watching the man at the table.

"How do you plan to proceed?" asked Grant.

"It would help if I knew *what* it is you think he knows."

Grant was about to speak when a bullet blasted through the small window on the interrogation room door, hitting Sam squarely in the forehead. The chair he was in fell backward from the force of the bullet and Sam lay lifeless on the floor.

Trevyn ran from observation and down the hall past the room where Sam now lay dead. Grant was right behind him, but whoever pulled the trigger was gone.

Chapter Twenty-Three

Chaos broke out as agents went in every direction trying to find the gunman. No one was seen entering or exiting the hallway from either end. The gunman had to have only seconds to disappear as Trevyn and Grant were immediately out the observation room door.

It was no use, the gunman escaped unseen. Grant went into tracking mode and slowly moved up and down the hall, trying to pick up a scent or a print. There were no prints, but there was a scent and he followed it down the hall, away from the main entrance and around the corner. Unfortunately, there were too many bodies searching the hallways and offices to follow any one scent, making it impossible to pinpoint the single scent. Frustrated, he returned to interrogation.

The body was just being removed and CSI had taken over the room and the hallway. "This way," said Trevyn, grabbing Grant's arm. They entered a small conference room and Trevyn closed the door.

"Were you able to find anything?"

"No, there were too many people coming and going. It mixed any scent I had found in with all the others."

"That's unfortunate. I should have thought about that and kept everyone out."

Grant shrugged and stared out the window. This was getting to be a really dirty investigation. And he really didn't like dirty.

"What are you thinking?" Trevyn had been watching Grant.

"I am not sure what to think. This is a secure building, is it not?"

"It is. Everyone goes through a checkpoint, just like at the airport."

"Then how did someone get in here with a gun, someone who was not an agent? It seems unlikely that could have happened, which leads me to only one conclusion. The Brevet organization has a man on the inside. He or she is one of yours."

"There has to be another conclusion. I can't believe we have a mole in the FBI. It just can't be."

"It has happened before, many times. Why are you so sure it could not happen in your office?"

"I…I don't know. It just…" Trevyn's voice trailed off and he collapsed into a chair. "It's just never happened *here* before."

Grant's cell phone rang and he took the call.

"Mulvane. Yes…yes…slow down. Who is this? Raina? This is Raina? Where are you? No, no, we will come to you. We will be there in five minutes."

Grant ended the call and stared at Trevyn. "That was Raina. She is at the shop. She said they told her we were looking for her, but she is safe. We need to find out where she was."

The two men hurried outside to the car. Neither spoke as they drove, both lost in thoughts of the shooting at the FBI office, the chance of a mole, and Raina suddenly showing up with not a care in the world. The car pulled up in front of the building and Grant and Trevyn started into the shop. The technicians had formed a line, blocking their entrance. They stood where they were, as if daring Grant to try to pass.

"You have Raina? She is here? She is safe?"

"It's okay guys. Let him through." The line parted and Raina sat on the hood of a car. She looked worn and tired.

"What has happened, Raina? Where have you been?"

"I...I needed some time, I needed to think, so I took a couple of days to figure things out."

Trevyn came up behind Grant. Grant could feel his surprise, and heard the tension in his voice. "That is *not* Raina."

Raina looked at him in surprise. "If I'm not me, then who am I? What do you mean I'm not Raina?"

Grant stared at Trevyn. Trevyn whispered quickly and evenly. "Say nothing. We need to talk. Bring her."

Grant stood between Trevyn and Raina. "Can you come with us? We have much to discuss."

"I...I guess so. I feel bad for causing all the fuss. I should have called you and Sam. I just have been off my game since Jimmy disappeared. I need time to think. Where's Sam?"

Trevyn gave a very sparse shake of his head to Grant. Grant turned back to Raina. "We can talk about that. Are you okay to come with us?"

There were murmurs among the other technicians until one man stepped forward. "What has happened to Sam? We have a right to know. He's our boss."

Trevyn's eyes met those of the technician. "We will tell you what we can when we can. Right now, we don't have any answers for you."

"What do you mean you don't have any answers? He left with *you*, and he was in *handcuffs*."

"Listen, everyone. There has been a shooting at the field office; that's all I can tell you. There are a lot of things that need to be sorted out. If there is a supervisor who can take over things temporarily, then he or she should take charge. I will get back to you as soon as I can. For right now, please, just be patient."

There was a stunned silence from the workers as Grant, Raina, and Trevyn left the shop. Grant helped Raina into the backseat and he got into the passenger seat.

"Where are you taking me?" Raina's voice was shaky. "Have I done something wrong?"

"No, Raina, you have done nothing wrong." Grant spoke softly to calm her nerves. "We need to ask you some questions, that is all. Are you okay with that?"

"Yes…yes. Anything I can do to help."

They pulled up in front of the field office and parked the car. They entered the office and went directly into the conference room on the other side of the building from where Sam had been shot. Trevyn didn't want Raina to see the crime scene before he had a chance to explain things to her.

As they sat down, he started right in. "Raina, we picked up Sam today and took him to the field office for questioning. However, before we could interview him, someone shot him and then escaped."

"Is he...is he going to be okay?"

"No, I'm sorry to have to tell you, Sam is dead."

"Sam? Sam is dead? I thought this was the FBI? I thought you guys protected people? How could this happen?" Raina's reaction confirmed to Trevyn that she knew nothing of the shooting, a concern he'd kept to himself. Her eyes were fearful and her hands were shaking. She rested one hand on her belly, as if protecting the little person growing there.

Trevyn continued. "We're trying to find that out right now. Are you okay to answer a few questions?"

"Yes. But...why would anyone want to kill Sam? He was...a little a bit secretive, but I don't think that was enough to *kill* him for."

"Obvious, someone did. We're investigating that now. We're not sure what his part in all of this is, but we'll get it figured out. Now, first, tell me where you were for the last two days."

Raina was silent for a moment. "I was looking for Jimmy."

"So you didn't need to get away then. You just wanted to find Jimmy?"

"Not...not exactly. My family has a cabin up in the mountains. I'd originally planned to go there and try to figure out my head. I've been worried about Jimmy, I was feeling abandoned and alone. I was heartbroken. But when I thought about it, I realized I know Jimmy well enough to know that if he knew of our baby, he wouldn't stay away."

"Where did you look?"

"I just wandered. I didn't go to the cabin. I stayed in town and looked everywhere we'd ever been, any place we'd eaten, the movie theatre, the park. I searched everywhere I could think of."

"Okay, I understand."

Grant leaned in and rested his forearms on the table, clasping his hands in front of him. "Raina, did you know someone using your name was working with the FBI as an informant?"

"No, how would I know that? How long has she been working with you?" She turned from Grant to Trevyn. "Don't you guys ask for ID? She couldn't have given you any documents that proved she was me, unless they were faked."

"It wasn't like that. But now that we know she isn't you, we will have to figure out who she is. It does explain a lot, though, about why we didn't know about your relationship with Jimmy and about the baby."

Grant stepped in. "I wonder, Raina, if you should stay with Shannon for a while until we can get this whole thing sorted out. Can you agree to do that?"

"I have a place of my own, Grant. I'm perfectly fine to stay there."

"Yes, Raina, I am sure you are, but a woman, for some reason, is trying to make people think she is you. That raises concerns that you could be in danger. It makes me uncomfortable knowing you would be alone. And it is not just you anymore, Raina, you have a little one to look out for now."

"Raina," began Trevyn, "I think Grant has a good point. It would make our job a lot easier to know that you are safe. Maybe take some time off work for a few more days until we can get this figured out.

We'll post some agents outside Shannon's apartment complex to keep an eye on things."

"Okay, but are you sure this will be okay with Shannon?"

Grant smiled softly and patted her arm. "I feel fairly certain she will not have a problem with it."

Trevyn looked at the clock. "It's almost five. What time do you need to pick up Shannon?"

"I will ask you to take me over there now, if you are okay with that," Grant chuckled. "And you, Raina, are you okay to stay with Shannon for a few days? Can you let the shop know you'll be gone a few more days?"

"I would like that," she said, her hand still on her stomach. "We both would. And yes, I'll let the guys know I won't be in for a few days." Raina giggled softly at the thought of the child she carried. "It's hard to remember there's a little one in there," she said, moving her hand slowly over her stomach, "and that this little one needs me as much as I need him…or her."

They rose to go and left the conference room, heading to the car. Trevyn dropped both Raina and Grant off at Shannon's work, and they rode the elevator together to her floor.

Throughout the day, Grant had kept a picture in his mind and in his heart of a beautiful raven-haired woman working safely at her desk. Still, even with all the visual he had kept, seeing her there as they approached her office took his breath away. A wave of relief swept over him as he saw her working at her desk. There was so much to tell her, but for now, he just wanted to see her in her element, unaware of his coming.

As Raina and Grant came through her door Shannon looked up and that gorgeous smile slid effortlessly across her face.

"Raina! How nice to see you. Oh, and you, too, of course," she chuckled at Grant. She rose gracefully from her desk and walked around it, giving Raina a large hug.

"How would you like another house guest for a few days?"

Shannon's smile broadened. "Don't toy with me, Grant. Are you saying I get to have a sleepover with my new sister?" She looked expectantly at Raina.

"Are you sure you don't mind? I told them I was fine to stay at my apartment. I don't want to cause you any trouble."

"Are you *kidding me*? This is the stuff dreams are made of! We're going to have so much fun!"

Grant thought to himself, *I think I will do just fine with a hotel room. I have a feeling that is the only way I will get any rest.*

Chapter Twenty-Four

As hard as it was to leave Shannon when their time together was so limited, Grant found a nice hotel close to her apartment. He knew she needed the time with Raina, and as it turned out, Grant needed a solid block of time to meditate.

Grant took Shannon's SUV and if needed, they would get Raina's car, still parked at the shop, and Raina and Shannon could use that. However, the women were pretty much remanded to Shannon's place, with no coming or going allowed, so a car was not going to be necessary.

Trevyn had already made the arrangements for the agents who would stand guard at Shannon's apartment, and Grant felt a sense of relief when he saw their car parked in front of the complex.

Once he'd dropped the women at Shannon's, he headed to the hotel. He dropped his things on the bed and went immediately to a corner of the room and sat down cross-legged on the floor.

The meditation began as it usually did, but soon his thoughts were consumed with visions of Shannon at the picnic in Alaska, in the offices of the Alaska State Troopers…in his mind he saw all the emotions she'd experienced since she first made herself known in his barn that night; powerful, frightened, happy, crying; every emotion he had experienced with her filled his senses, denying him any chance of the soothing, organization of his thoughts for the day. He tried over and over again, to no avail.

    Finally, forcing his mind to put Shannon behind his other thoughts, he brought the events of the day to the front. Closing his eyes and breathing deeply, he created a small box for her essence, closed the box, and began his meditation for the day. It was the single most difficult meditation he'd ever experienced, but once he'd calmed himself he felt the relief that he so desperately needed.

    Someone was out there telling the FBI she was Raina. Do they not research the people they employ? Why would they not know she wasn't who she said she was? This made no sense. Raina went looking for Jimmy, though there was a nagging thought in the back of Grant's mind that there was more to this story than they were hearing from her. Then there was the killing of Sam. This presented not only one factor, but two. First, who would want to kill him; second, why? He seemed beloved by his employees, currying intense feelings from them of loyalty and protection. Protection? Why would their boss need protection? That emotion stood out stronger than the loyalty. He felt it intensely, almost like a fire that refused to be extinguished. Why?

    Grant's eyes popped open. He stood and went to the pocket of his coat and removed his cell phone. He dialed Trevyn and waited as the phone rang.

    "James."

"Trevyn, this is Grant. I need you to come to my hotel immediately."

"Grant, do you know what time it is?"

Grant's brain did the math and figured it was probably eight in the evening. He told Trevyn the time.

"Look at your watch, Grant."

"I do not wear a watch."

"Then look at a *clock*! It's 3 a.m."

The time had flown by, and Grant was stunned by the realization. "I...I am sorry. I had no idea."

"No worries. You really need me to come over there now? I will if you want me to."

"No, no, I need to get some sleep. I'll talk to you in the morning. I have to pick up Shannon in the morning and take her to work. I would like Raina there when we talk anyway. Let's meet up at the diner for breakfast again."

"I'll be there."

The call ended and Grant prepared himself for bed. As he slid under the covers and felt the crispness of the sheets, his mind remembered when Shannon would sleep on the other side of the bed. His arm reached out instinctively, and felt only emptiness there. She had managed to escape from the box he'd put her in, and now she filled his world once again. How did people get anything done when they felt such emotions for another person? How did they get any sleep at all? That was the last thought in his mind as his brain slipped gradually into sleep.

§§§

Shannon was beautiful, ready for work and all smiles. But there was a certain amount of sleep deprivation that showed in the eyes of both her and

Raina. Once Grant dropped her at work, he and Raina drove to the diner where Trevyn was already waiting for them.

Breakfast had not been ordered and after each of them gave their order to the waitress, Trevyn began. "Now, what was so urgent you had to wake me up at three o'clock in the morning?"

Raina's eyes widened. "You were up at three? You should have come over! You could have joined our party." She giggled at her offer. "Why were *you* up so late?"

"Let me answer your question with a question," began Grant. "Tell me about Sam. What was he like as a boss, and as a human being?"

Raina gazed out the window for a moment. "He was a good man, but he was a man with a lot of secrets. I don't know how to explain it. Recently, he began leaving the office to do what he called, a 'parts run.' But he'd always come back with nothing. He was so good to us as his employees. He often bought pizza for lunch and had it delivered. He would help us out if we couldn't make rent or needed a doctor visit, never asking for the money back. He let us use the shop any time we needed it to fix our cars. He was good to us. But…" Raina's voice trailed off and she returned to gazing out the window.

Grant nudged her gently. "But…?"

"If I didn't know better I'd say he was dealing drugs, but that's ridiculous. I thought he must have had some kind of business on the side. Sam became secretive, sneaking out of the shop at weird times of the day and often meeting with people in his office. He would close the blinds on the windows whenever they came in. Several weeks before he…left…Jimmy said he didn't think we should trust Sam anymore.

When I asked him why, he didn't answer. He only said, "Be careful."

Grant turned to Trevyn. "Last night when I was meditating-"

"Do you always meditate at three in the morning?" Trevyn smirked.

"Only when I do not know it is three in the morning. But last night...okay, this morning, it occurred to me that Sam's employees were not just loyal to the man, they were *protective* of him. This at least gives us some information we did not have before."

Trevyn had listened intently to the exchange. "We need to know where Sam went when he left the shop for those parts runs. I'm not sure we'll ever know, now that he's dead."

Grant turned again to Raina. "Was Jimmy aware of these times that Sam would leave the office during the work day?"

"Somewhat. At least enough to make him suspicious," Raina's voice grew soft, "but a lot of those meetings and strange runs to the parts store started after Jimmy left."

Grant looked at Trevyn, whose eyes were wide with sudden understanding. "Sam wasn't killed because of what he knew, he was killed because of what he *didn't* know."

"What are you talking about?" Raina's voice was more fearful. "You're not making sense."

"Raina," said Trevyn, "I know these questions sound strange, but if you could just answer them for us, I will make sure you are filled in on what his role was with the FBI, and what we know now. Can you tell me...how long after Jimmy disappeared did these parts runs become a regular activity for Sam?"

"Probably a week or two. I don't know…I didn't really pay attention. I just remember seeing him leaving more often, more regularly, after Jimmy was gone."

"Trevyn, how long was Jimmy working with the FBI before he disappeared?" asked Grant.

"Probably about eight months or so. He disappeared from our radar a month ago."

"And Raina, how long ago was it that Jimmy became secretive about the comings and goings of the two of you?" Grant's eyes were determined, searching.

"Maybe…" Grant could almost hear her wheels turning. "Maybe four month ago. But I can't be sure; I had no reason to worry about that. I didn't know all of this was going on. And I certainly didn't know he was working for the FBI."

The group sat quietly while the waitress delivered their breakfasts. Raina had only a bowl of dry Cheerios. Her stomach didn't seem to allow anything else into it in the mornings.

"Here is what I think," began Grant. "The Brevet organization contacted Sam and possibly asked some favor of him, for which they paid him generously. It could be that whatever the favor was, it was about Jimmy. Though Sam knew nothing of what Jimmy was up to, and knew nothing of the organization, when he was brought into the FBI for questioning, the Brevet couldn't risk him saying something he may have seen or heard, or tell them anything about their request for information regarding Jimmy. He became a liability."

"Who are these people?" Raina's eyes were wide and anxious.

Trevyn studied her face as he responded. "They are people that will do anything to get what they want. *Anything.*"

Chapter Twenty-Five

The group finished their breakfasts, and Grant took Raina to the shop. Trevyn followed in his car. Grant then drove to Shannon's office and parked the SUV in her designated spot. He exited the car and locked the doors; pocketing the Shannon's of keys she'd given him that morning. There was a sense of comfort knowing the car was there, but Shannon didn't have keys to drive it anywhere, should she be tempted to leave the office building. Trevyn pulled up behind the parked SUV and waited for Grant to get in.

As Grant slid into the passenger seat and shut the door, Trevyn held out a slip of torn paper with a short note scrawled across the front of it. Trevyn pulled out of the parking lot and started down the street as Grant read the note.

"2259 Kroeker St."

"What is this?" Grant held the paper up to the light to see if there was something he was missing.

"It's an address."

Grant gave Trevyn a flat stare. "Yes, I can see that. What does it mean?"

Trevyn chuckled and took the note back. "It's the address of a street with a row of large warehouses on it."

"The Brevet own warehouses."

"That's what I was thinking," smiled Trevyn as he pulled up to a red light.

"Where did you get the note?"

"It was on the front seat of my *locked* car this morning."

"Hmm," said Grant. "I guess we should check this out. But how do we do that without the organization *knowing* we're doing that."

"I'll show you," replied Trevyn. The light turned green and they proceeded down the street.

They turned a corner just before Kroeker Street and pulled up in front of a dilapidated old apartment building. Grant followed Trevyn inside and to the manager's office. An elderly gentleman with shaky hands gave them the keys to one of the third floor apartments, and they proceeded up the stairs.

"I don't trust the elevator," smirked Trevyn.

Arriving on the third floor, it was far more obvious just how old this building was. Paint was peeling from the walls and door jams, and the doorknobs and hinges were badly rusted. They proceeded down the hallway to number thirty-two and Trevyn opened the door.

The one room apartment was vacant. Grant was certain this was a good thing as there was rat excrement in just about every corner. The smell was almost more than he could stand, but he forced himself to separate it from his thoughts and followed Trevyn to the only piece of furniture in the room.

Near a window with a thin, hole-ridden, lace drape, stood a camera on a tripod, with a large telephoto lens. Next to the camera were two worn kitchen style chairs with about the same amount of rust as the hardware on all the apartment doors. The camera appeared to already be pointed down to the street below.

Trevyn explained as he sat down in the chair and peeked into the camera. "I called the office as soon as I found the note and asked them to find out what was on the street. I told them if they thought it was anything noteworthy, to get a room set up."

Grant stared across the street to the large older warehouse. "Why are we watching this one? I do not believe Jimmy is in this one."

Trevyn eyed Grant warily. "How would you know that?"

Grant ignored the question and repeated himself. "Why are we watching this one?"

"We're actually watching all of them. We don't know which one he is in, or if he is in any of these. Since we don't know where the note came from that directed us here, we're not even sure he's here. We're simply making an assumption."

Grant walked to the window, keeping himself hidden behind the walls that separated each one. He slowly lifted the edge of one filthy curtain and peered outside, his eyes searching the street and buildings below.

Trevyn watched him from his chair. "You said you didn't believe Jimmy was in the warehouse in front of us. How can you know that?"

Grant continued to watch the street. "I am a tracker. However, I do not use only my eyes when I track. The gift the Spirits gave me comes from inside of me first. I *feel* things, from inside me, before I ever begin physically tracking something or someone."

"So, your gut tells you if something is there."

Grant turned his attention from the street to Trevyn, his eyes thoughtful. "No, my 'guts' do not speak to me. Only the Spirits speak to me and the feeling comes from inside of me, from a place that cannot be influenced by outside events. I can tell you of a surety that Jimmy is not in this warehouse," he said, nodding to the building across the street. "He is in that one," he said pointing to the building next to it. "He is hurt, and is currently being tended to by another man. That man is frightened. He is there against his will."

"Oh, come on. You'd have to be psychic to know that. You can't *know* that."

"I cannot explain to you how I know that. I guess you could say it is more like I am being told by my soul that this is so. And it helps that the smell outside that building is wrong."

Trevyn was quickly becoming cynical. "Right. And you would have smelled this when?"

"When I exited your car."

"So, you could smell this 'wrong' odor from nearly a half a block away?"

"You are correct."

Trevyn could see that Grant's disposition had changed. More than changed. It had done an about-face. His eyes were narrow and focused, his shoulders at attention and his speech was formal, more so than was normal for him. There was something in the way he stood at the window that made Trevyn feel Grant's honesty. But Trevyn was having a difficult time wrapping his head around the man's explanations.

"I know it is difficult to believe me, I know you are having a hard time digesting what I am telling you. However, if you choose to not act, you will lose the window of opportunity that has been given us by that note. Time is short. You must move quickly."

Trevyn stood and moved in beside Grant. "I can't tell the Bureau I need a raid on a warehouse without more than what you're telling me. I need evidence. I need to see people moving in and out of the building. I need photos, taped conversations, bodies, *anything*. Just something that I can take to my boss that says I need a warrant."

Grant shrugged and smiled at Trevyn. "I can only tell you what I know."

The two men stood beside the window, watching the street below. A car drove slowly up to the warehouse and turned down an alleyway between the two warehouses.

"Now, see? *That's* what I need. Let's go see what they're doing, shall we?"

They left the apartment, locking the door behind them. Hurrying down the stairs, Grant and Trevyn continued out the back door of the complex. There was an alley between the two large buildings that sat beside the apartments, directly across from the one they were watching. Grant and Trevyn crept into the alley, keeping low and close to the wall. From their vantage point, they watched as two men came out of the building and entered the parked sedan, one into the driver's seat, the other into the passenger's seat.

The large black sedan pulled forward in the alley and out onto the street behind the warehouse. Trevyn was obviously disappointed.

"Well, that was a whole lot of nothing," he said.

"The warehouse looks empty. I do not think there are any businesses inside."

"Yes, we've already looked into that. Neither of these two warehouses are advertised for rent or sale, according to the agents I had looking into the address on the note in my car this morning."

"When did you have time to set that up? We were at the restaurant pretty early."

"Yes, true, but while I waited for you and Raina, I put in the call to my office, and as I was following you to drop off Raina and then Shannon's car, I received the call back from the agent at the office. He filled me in on the specs of the warehouse and we made all the set-up arrangements then."

"Impressive."

The men returned to the apartment building and up to their room. Grant had the distinct feeling it was going to be a long day.

To break up some of the monotony, they decided to take the camera from the tripod and bring it down to the same alley they were in earlier. If anyone came or went from that alley, they would be ready with the camera.

It was nearing two o'clock when another car drove into the alley. Grant and Trevyn watched with interest as two men exited the car and the driver opened the passenger door behind the driver's seat. The man reached in and grabbed what looked like an arm. His eyes focused on the driver, Grant was not prepared for what he would see next. As the person was pulled from the back seat, his heart seemed to stop beating, his breath frozen in his chest.

Attempting to pull her arm free of her captors grip, Shannon stumbled from the car. Grant's mind worked to understand what he was seeing. *It was Shannon*. His Shannon. Grant's response was instantaneous. Without any further thought, his mind whirled into attack mode, attempting to fly over the debris they were hiding behind. He hadn't moved more than an inch when Trevyn quickly and silently pulled him back down.

"Now I can call for back up...*and* a warrant."

Chapter Twenty-Six

Grant could feel all his grandfather's training, his years of mediations, the quiet discipline that ruled his life, all of it, slipping away. It was as if he was suddenly on a giant waterslide moving out of control to the water below.

Trevyn still had a wad of Grant's shirt in his hand, holding him in place. It was all Grant could do to not drop him where he stood and run for the warehouse. He knew this would be a wrong choice and sat back against the wall, breathing slowly, deeply, and praying for the help he would need to calm his spirit.

He closed his eyes and thought about the morning he and his grandfather had found the elk and the peace he felt in that moment. The confidence with which he'd given the instruction to walk carefully, to the man who'd taught him all he knew. The surety he felt in what he'd said in that moment.

The peace came flooding back to him and his body calmed, his mind came back into focus and he could think again, his thoughts clear and concise. He knew without this calm, he would be useless to Shannon and could even get her killed. Grant knew he must think through each step, plan his actions and keep Shannon safe.

Trevyn was on his cell phone calling for backup and explaining the probable cause that would allow them to enter the warehouse without waiting for a warrant. His voice was strong and controlled, yet urgent.

Unable to see into the warehouse, neither man had any idea what to expect. The only entry and exit they'd seen was the two same men who'd just taken Shannon inside the building. Were there more men in there? How many more? What kind of guns were they carrying? What was the layout of the warehouse?

Trevyn ordered an immediate floor plan for the warehouse. He ordered bulletproof vests for both himself and Grant. He explained that the arrival of backup had to be covert, that they couldn't alert the people inside the building to their presence.

Once he was sure he'd covered all the ifs he could think of, Trevyn ended the call and turned his attention back to Grant.

"Are you okay? I thought I was going to lose you there for a while."

"I am fine. I just needed to…get my bearings. I will not lose focus again. What is the plan?"

Grant could feel the calm inside him, like morning fog over a perfectly still pond. Before Trevyn could respond, thoughts formed into words and poured quickly, yet controlled, from Grant's mouth.

"Jimmy is not doing well. There is a man tending to him, he must be a doctor, he…knows things…"

"He what?" Trevyn wasn't sure what Grant was telling him.

"He knows what to do to help Jimmy, he could be a physician, but he is in fear for his life. He is there against his will; however, his main focus is on Jimmy. The room they are in has a very high ceiling; it is large and empty. Shannon is confused, but safe. She does not know Jimmy is in the same building. Jimmy is not aware that Shannon has arrived. There is much fear in that building, and much evil."

Trevyn was stunned. "You can tell that from out here?"

"I can *smell* that from out here."

"Can you tell me how many are in the building?"

"Not for sure, but there are not more than ten, probably less. That count would include Shannon, Jimmy and the man tending him."

Trevyn was trying very hard to believe what Grant was saying. Grant felt his struggle.

"I understand your doubt. I am not offended. I do not ask that you believe me, I only tell you what I know is true. Whether or not you decide to act on what I tell you is a choice you must make. However, it is important for you to know that the woman I love is being held in that building against her will. I, too, have choices to make, and my choices will be directly influenced by yours."

"I'm not entirely sure," said Trevyn, glancing tentatively at Grant. "But, did you just threaten me?"

"No. I was simply stating the facts as I know them, so you, too, can know my intentions."

"Right. Now you're just confusing me."

Grant wasn't smiling; his eyes studied every inch of the warehouse across the street. Every muscle in his body was tight, serpent-like, ready to strike. He wasn't going to waste valuable time explaining himself. He was focused and ready to act. But he wasn't a fool. He would wait for the right time, and when that time came, he would do what must be done.

Two agents, a man and a woman, approached from behind Trevyn and Grant in the alley. They were bent over and staying close to the wall.

"Just us," whispered the woman. "What have you got?"

"Hey, Lyn," said Trevyn softly. This is Grant Mulvane, Grant, meet Lyn; behind her is Boris…his real name is Harley, but we call him Boris. They're agents with the Bureau from my field office."

Grant had his mind elsewhere, but was polite and shook both their hands, returning quickly to his study of the warehouse, and any other scents that he could pick up. Some of the intense feelings were coming from both Shannon and Jimmy. Still separated, their feelings were not angry, not frightened, and different from each other. Jimmy was mourning, his heart was broken, Shannon was concerned, her heart was racing, yet he could feel her calming herself, slowly forcing herself to relax.

Grant began checking for open doors or windows. There had to be a place that these scents were escaping from. Generally, it was beyond his abilities to track anything through a closed building. There had to be an opening. He turned to Trevyn.

"There is a door open somewhere close to the ground, or maybe a window, but it would be quite a large window. Someone has either left it open by accident or meant to do so. I believe it was the latter."

Lyn stared at Trevyn with a look of puzzlement on her face. "What did he say?"

Boris had the same look and glanced from Trevyn to Grant and back to Trevyn.

"You heard the man," said Trevyn. "We need to find that door."

Several more agents converged on the alley where Grant and Trevyn were. They were given the same instructions as Lyn and Boris. They melted into the alley and out onto the street behind Grant and Trevyn's position.

"I cannot do any more from out here. I must get inside that building." Grant never took his eyes from the looming warehouse and alley across the street.

"You can't go in there, Grant. Let my people take care of the inside of the warehouse. You just keep feeding me anything you can."

"There is no more information I can get from out here. I am going inside."

Trevyn grabbed Grant's arm to keep him down. Grant turned his attention to Trevyn, his eyes were piercing and unyielding. There was a determination in them that Trevyn hadn't seen until now. This was a man who was not to be trifled with. Something told Trevyn things would go better if he let Grant do what he needed to do. He released his hold and rose from his crouched position.

"Fine. But I'm going with you."

"That is an excellent choice." The two men moved back through the alley and to the street. The Brevet was about to get a giant dose of Grant Mulvane.

Chapter Twenty-Seven

Shannon's day started out the same as the days before. She'd been back only a couple days, but it was good to have a routine to stick to. She needed her routine. And she trusted Grant to do what he needed to do. Still...she worried about Jimmy. It was hard not to.

Her eyes traveled around the room to the two "staffers" who were looking busy filing and organizing the day. Shannon only hoped she would be able to find her client files once this whole fiasco was over.

She looked at her pathetic sack lunch and wondered if the nightmare ever would be over. The lunch in that brown bag was the least she could do to keep Grant from worrying about where she was eating and if she was safe outside the walls of her office. She shook her head with a sad smile. She loved Grant. She knew she loved him. She was certain his feelings for her were as strong, wasn't she?

The smile faded from her lips. She shook herself free of the doubt and dropped the lunch bag into the drawer at her desk. She sat down and proceeded through the files, checking off what had been done, circling the items that needed attention. She then organized the files by need and started in on them.

When she looked at the clock it was almost eleven, and she had to get to the bathroom fast. The time had flown, and with all the water she'd been sipping, her bladder was issuing a code red warning.

She hurried to the restroom. She could hear the agents behind her, rushing to catch up. As she went inside, the two agents waited in the hallway on either side of the door, chatting like girlfriends. Shannon grinned. They were good at what they did. She wondered if they shouldn't try some theater in their off hours.

Shannon was washing her hands when she heard a thud in the hallway and the restroom door flew open. Two men rushed her and one placed his hand over her mouth before the air in her lungs could push the scream from her voice box. His hand held a piece of cloth with a substance that smelled horrible, but Shannon couldn't help but breath in the fumes.

Whisked from the room, she barely had time to wonder if the two still bodies of her guards, lying on the floor in the hallway, were alive or dead. She could only hope they were going to be okay. She wasn't sure she would be. The hallway began to swim, but her abductors held her fast and rushed her outside.

Shoved into the backseat of a dark sedan, Shannon tried to fight back, but whatever they'd done to her made her muscles weak. She was completely coherent, but unable to fight back. Was this what they'd done to Jimmy? Is this how they took him?

The car left the parking lot behind her building just as several police cruisers pulled up to the front.

Law enforcement flowed into the building, but Shannon knew they wouldn't find her there, maybe they would never find her.

She could almost hear Grant's voice in her head, instructing her to breathe in through her nose, deeply, and blow out through her mouth. She did this several times, trying not to think about where they were taking her or why, but keeping herself in the moment.

Whatever they'd given her had to have a very short-term effect because with the breathing, the world around her stopped spinning, her world coming back into focus. Opening her eyes barely enough to see, she studied the two men in the front seat. She reached slowly, covertly, for the door handle. She pulled it toward her but nothing happened. One of her abductors looked at the other and smiled sarcastically. "Looks like the *princess* is moving."

Shannon knew it was pointless to try to escape. She kept breathing, continued to clear her lungs and her head. She made no effort to communicate with her captors, nor did they try to speak to her.

She thought of Grant, of what he would be telling her to do right now. Stay calm, keep breathing, and focus, and that is exactly what she did. Shannon began organizing her thoughts like they were files on her desk. Methodically and practically, she thought through her situation.

If Jimmy were dead, this Brevet organization would have no need for her. Shannon was certain Jimmy was still alive, and this was a good thing. If they were going to use her as leverage to get Jimmy to do what they needed him to do, like Tope and Sawyer had talked about, then they were probably taking her to the same place they were holding Jimmy.

Shannon's stomach dropped at the next thought. If they were going to use her as coercion for Jimmy, they would probably kill her. She tossed that thought. It made no sense and only caused her stomach to constrict, along with her lungs and throat. Not helpful.

Once she'd arranged her thoughts as best she could, there was only one thing to do. She waited. Shannon said nothing; she just waited to see what came next. Whatever it was, she would handle it.

Shannon couldn't help the small smile that slid across her face. She'd been around Grant too long. All this calming and thinking was working in the face of uncertainty. And it truly did help. If she ever saw him again, she would tell him how helpful he was to her.

The thought of not seeing Grant again, of not seeing her brother again, and of never having a chance to hold her new niece or nephew...those things stole the calm that she'd been feeling. It wasn't as if she was no longer calm, it was more that, now, she was angry. These men were trying to steal her family from her, and that was not okay.

Her thoughts changed from checklist to fight list. She would fight her way out of this if she had to, and it appeared she had to.

The car pulled up in front of a dilapidated old warehouse in the industrial part of Smithville. The area used to be a large staging area where trains dropped their shipments to major suppliers of businesses in the city. With the loss of the train system, the warehouses quickly went silent, and were soon forgotten by the town.

Obviously, not everyone had forgotten about them, because she was now being pulled from the back seat and forced inside the warehouse. Her hands were not tied, and she decided not to waste the strength that had been slowly returning to her body. Once inside the door, she elbowed the man on her right and her knee went right to the groin of the man on her left. Her left side became free and she tried to shove the man she'd elbowed, but she didn't have quite that much strength. He was a big, and towered over her threateningly.

She felt his hand grab her hair and force her head back. His breath smelled of old beer and stale cigarettes, but she forced her face to remain blank.

"Listen lady, you do what I say and he might let you live. You pull a stunt like this again, and I'll make sure he doesn't."

The man had a strong hold of her arm and held it behind her back. She was forced down a hallway, into a small dirty room filled with oversized storage boxes. The large man shoved her, causing her to stumble into the boxes and land in the middle of them. He slammed the door and she could hear him lock it from the outside. At least he'd left the light on.

Her first thought was to try to find something in the boxes that could be useful in her escape, but with each box she opened, that thought slowly died. There was nothing in them but old files.

Shannon started in on another box, just to be sure, when she heard the lock on the door. She stopped what she was doing and quickly turned to face whoever was coming through. She prayed it was Grant and Trevyn, but it was not. It was the same man who put her in the room, and from the look in his eyes, he was about to take her out.

Chapter Twenty-Eight

Grant moved with a fluid motion that kept Trevyn working to keep up. He seemed to blend into his surroundings, moving in sync with objects around him. Something about the way his body flowed made Trevyn wonder if anyone could actually see him, which he knew was ridiculous. Trevyn could definitely see him, but he was moving with him, working with him. He'd never experienced anything like this.

Grant went two blocks down the street from where the warehouse in question stood. He crossed over to the same side of the street as the building, and then went one block further, enabling him to come in from behind the structure.

If there were cars or people, dogs or cats, anything living at all, Grant paid no attention. He was a man on a mission, and his intent drove him forward, planning his moves with precision. His mind was focused only on Shannon. He knew where she was, and where Jimmy would be as well. How he knew this was a mystery to Trevyn.

§§§

Grant stopped with no warning. It was as if the world stopped, as if nothing existed but he and the building before him. His heart beat strong and sure in his ears. Something was wrong inside the warehouse.

Following close behind Grant, Trevyn nearly ran into him when he stopped so abruptly. "What? What's wrong?"

"Can you contact your team?"

"Yes, I have a handheld."

"Something is happening. Both Shannon and Jimmy are in danger. We must get inside now. Right now."

Just at that moment, the radio handheld crackled and Lyn spoke. "We've found the open door. It leads into the back of the warehouse. We're going in."

"Wait," responded Trevyn. "We're seconds behind you. Wait for us before entering."

"Roger that."

Grant broke into a run and raced to the back of the warehouse. The team of six agents, led by Lyn and Boris, crouched outside the door, in a covered, recessed entryway hidden from the street.

They entered the building single file, each in his turn checking both ways into the hallway they entered. All was quiet, but there were voices coming from the main room.

Grant moved quickly, stealthily, to the head of the line. He hid himself beside the doorway leading into the large open room. Several agents followed him, the rest lining up on the opposite side of the door.

Grant's eyes quickly scanned the part of the room he could see.

There were three men in the room standing against the far wall to the right of the entry. The men had guns in holsters and they chatted casually together. Just inside and lined up about three feet from the wall, on both sides of the door, stood a single row of fifty-gallon drums. Grant silently questioned the intellect of the abductors. Surely, they would know how this simplified a rescue. He thanked the Spirits for the ignorance of these men.

Trevyn's face took on a sense of surprised betrayal. He motioned to the others that he'd found the mole and to stay quiet. One of the three men leaning against the far wall and talking together was Noal Drummond, an agent with their field office. Now he had an answer to the question of who'd shot Sam. The idea that one of his agents could be any part of this sickened his stomach. Trevyn struggled to maintain control. This was going to be a shock to the team.

Trevyn motioned for the team to begin entering the room, one by one, hiding behind the drums. Silently pointing to the team members, he directed them to their places.

Trevyn and Grant were the last to go in. The drums they were hiding behind had blocked the view of the filthy mattress Jimmy was laying on, and once inside the men could see them through the cracks between the containers. The man Grant assumed was a physician, sat next to Jimmy, looking worn and weary. Grant took in every inch of the warehouse, the people, their scents, the positioning of everyone, who had guns, who didn't have guns.

With the same silent signals as before, Trevyn sent out their plan of attack. His instructions were interrupted by the sound of Shannon's voice.

"JIMMY!"

"Shannon? Is that you? It can't be! They said you were dead!"

Grant watched as Shannon ran to Jimmy and fell on her knees beside him. That seemed to be a signal to the three men leaning against the wall. They pulled their guns and slowly began walking toward their captives.

One of the three men, apparently their leader, began talking as they approached Jimmy, Shannon, and the doctor. He addressed Jimmy with a cruel smile on his face.

"We'd planned to kill her a while ago, but then I had a wonderful thought. Why not do it in front of you, Jimmy? That way, you could know for sure that she was, indeed, dead." The man tipped his head toward Noal, who approached Shannon and pulled her to her feet. Holding her tightly to him, he placed the barrel of his gun against the side of her head.

Shannon gasped and froze in place, her dark eyes wide with fear. Grant could feel that fear. They were only a few feet from where he crouched behind the barrels. He had to think, he couldn't allow his emotions to drive him. Shannon's life depended on it.

Grant closed his eyes. He shut out Jimmy's screams and pleadings. He shut out the echo of those cries pulsing through the huge room. With his eyes closed, he steadied his breath and centered himself. With a rush of adrenalin, the room exploded into chaos.

Chapter Twenty-Nine

Grant watched as Jimmy pulled a gun from under him and fired in one swift movement. The man holding the gun on Shannon fell to the ground, and Shannon collapsed in shock and horror.

Grant was over the barrels in an instant. Bullets flew around him, one of them grazed his arm, but his motion never stopped. He flew over the mattress, over Jimmy, and planted his feet squarely into the chest of the traitor, who was still standing. Both Grant and Noal landed on their backs with a thud. Grant hit the floor in front of Shannon.

The traitor began to rise up, his gun trained on Grant. Trevyn fired and hit him in the chest. He fell back, not moving.

Shannon's emotions hit Grant as hard as the bullet that hit her captor. Her brother had just killed a man right in front of her, saving her life. But it seemed he'd done it without thinking, without even an ounce of guilt, and without hesitation. The revulsion Shannon felt at what she'd just experienced was followed by incredible guilt for feeling that revulsion. *Her brother had saved her life*, but where had he learned to kill with such confidence and precision? She was filled with dread as she sat on the floor gaping at the man she'd once known as her brother. Who was he now?

Within seconds, the gunfire ceased. The three abductors lay dead on the floor. Shannon was barely breathing, the look on her face moved from relief to loathing, to wonder, to shock. Her eyes remained locked with Jimmy's.

Grant rose quickly to his knees and wrapped both arms around Shannon. He placed his mouth next to her ear and whispered softly, penetrating the chaos of the room, "He saved your life, Shannon. For right now, this minute, *that* is what is important. He saved your life. He did what he had to do. Focus on that, shut out everything else. Focus."

Jimmy's reaction to his sister's shame and disgust for what he'd just done was frozen on his face. Unable to move his eyes from his sister, he stared back at Shannon, his face pleading for her understanding.

Shannon appeared almost catatonic, her breathing nearly nonexistent. Grant took her face in both his hands. "Look at me. Don't look at him, Shannon, look at me." He patted her face softly to get her attention. "Think, focus."

Slowly Shannon's eyes turned to him in soft lurching motions. When she saw him, she gasped and filled her lungs with air. Grant pulled her to him again and held her tightly.

"Shan…Shan…please…I'm sorry…" Jimmy's voice was gravelly and pain-filled. "They left me no choice! I couldn't let him kill you, I had to do shoot, Shan, I had to stop him."

He didn't look much like himself yet. He was less swollen, but bruises still covered his face and eyes.

The pleading in his voice was sure. He loved his sister. He'd done what had to be done. But in that voice, Grant heard something else. He would take that shot again if he had to, to save Shannon.

The man who'd attended Jimmy had been lost in the melee, but was now rising from having thrown himself on the floor to avoid stray bullets. He quickly checked his patient for bullet wounds. There were none.

"This man needs a hospital, though I'm not sure at this point it will do any good," he said to anyone who would listen. "He's needed a hospital from the moment I was brought here."

Trevyn stepped to his side. His green eyes were soft with thanks for what the man had done for Jimmy. He did his best to reassure him. "You did a very good thing here. I know it couldn't have been easy. We've already called for medical assistance. They should be here momentarily. Thank you for helping Jimmy."

The doctor nodded and returned to doing what he could for his patient.

A woman stepped silently from the shadows, the sound of her shoes echoing through the warehouse. Trevyn quickly lifted his gun, along with five other agents. The woman raised her hands. "Whoa. I'm one of the good guys. It's me, Agent James."

"Raina?" Trevyn put his gun into his holster and the others did the same. "What are you *doing* here?"

"Actually, the name is Hatch, and let me see…hmmm…what am I doing here…." The sarcasm in her voice didn't go unnoticed. "I've left notes on the seat of *locked* cars, I've left the warehouse door open for you to get inside, I've given a gun to young

Jimmy, there, and I've stayed out of the way of an FBI operation."

Trevyn chuckled. "I see. So, let me guess. You're not an informant for the FBI, and your first name is *not* Raina."

"Both true," she said smiling, as she reached inside her coat pocket. "I'm getting my ID, don't shoot me." She chuckled and pulled her credentials, displaying them for Trevyn.

Trevyn stared at the ID. "You're...you're CIA? What in the world is the CIA doing in Smithville, Iowa, Agent Hatch? This isn't CIA worthy."

"Oh, but it is, and call me Angela. This organization started selling arms to groups in the Middle East. They were quickly becoming more dangerous overseas than what they were doing here at home. We've been monitoring their communications for some time." She smiled and continued, "Oh, and I should tell you that I figured if I took Raina's name, they would be looking for me instead of her. It worked. They came after me alright, and locked me in a room over there," she pointed casually over her shoulder with her thumb to another entrance, "for about three minutes. You'll find another one of these in there," she said pointing to the dead bodies. "Only, he's not dead...but he probably wishes he were."

Trevyn chuckled. "Somehow, I'm thinking you're being modest."

Angela laughed. "I suppose I am. You may want to make sure there is more than one ambulance on the way."

"There is."

As if on cue, the sound of sirens began to penetrate the inside of the warehouse.

"This man goes first," said Jimmy's caregiver. "My name is Polson, Doctor Harriman Polson."

Trevyn reached out and shook his hand. "Thank you for your help today, Dr. Polson. I'll make sure he's the first one out."

Jimmy was trying to stay conscious now, and though it took great effort, he looked desperate to talk to Shannon.

"Shannon," his voice was a hoarse whisper.

Still locked in Grant's arms, Shannon felt the horror and shock gradually soften. Still unsure what to say to this man she no longer knew for sure, Grant gave her one last bit of advice. "Talk to him, Shannon. He will need your love and your support to heal from his wounds." He stood and moved back.

Shannon stared at Grant for only a moment before leaning over her brother. She looked into his eyes, and her heart softened. Tears formed in her eyes. Grant was right, they would sort all this out later. She carefully kissed her brother's cheek. "I'm here, Jimmy. I've prayed for this day, the day I would see you again. I will stay with you. I love you."

Finally, at the end of his pain threshold, Jimmy's eyes rolled back in his head and then closed. The EMTs were coming through the door with a gurney.

"Here," called Dr. Polson. "Take this man first. He needs immediate attention. I'm a doctor and I'll go with him."

"I'm his sister," said Shannon. I'm going with him, as well."

From the look on her face, no one dared argue with her about how many could be in the ambulance. She was going and that was that.

Shannon shot a glance at Grant. He smiled. "I'm right behind you."

"Grant! You've been hit!" Shannon gasped and took his arm carefully, inspecting the wound she'd not seen.

"I was only grazed. It is barely bleeding, Shannon. I am sure they will check it out at the hospital." She hugged him gently. "Now, go. Jimmy needs to get to the hospital. I will be fine. I will even let Trevyn drive me there."

"Promise?"

"I never lie."

The tears, still in her eyes, rolled down her cheeks. "No…no you don't."

§§§

The days at the hospital were long and grueling. Jimmy had severe internal bleeding. Dr. Polson had requested, early on, to continue with Jimmy's care. He spoke with Shannon the first day.

"I have no idea what kept this boy alive, Ms. Norton. Internal hemorrhaging like this is very unforgiving and fatal in nearly every instance. Whatever it was that kept him alive, it was strong and served its purpose. If he keeps up as he has, he will be okay. But these things have a nasty habit of turning bad corners. I don't want to get your hopes up, but whatever happens, you can be sure this boy is a fighter."

Grant stood beside Shannon with one arm around her. He gave her a squeeze as the doctor walked away. "He will be fine, Shannon."

Over the next few days, Jimmy's condition worsened, then bettered, then worsened several times.

Each time he came out of it and Dr. Polson marveled. It wasn't until the fourth day that Jimmy opened his eyes for the first time and smiled weakly at Shannon, her head on the bed, sound asleep. Her hand rested gently over Jimmy's hand. Grant was in the chair, also asleep. Jimmy moved his finger and Shannon jumped to attention.

"Jimmy?" She whispered. "Jimmy? Are you awake?"

Without waiting for an answer, she pushed the button calling for the nurses station. She could hear foot falls as the medical team raced down the hall.

"I'm awake," he whispered. "And you're alive."

Shannon smiled, feeling joy come all the way up from her toes. "Thanks to *you*, I'm alive."

Jimmy managed a weak smile before the medical team came through the door. The brought a rolling tray of equipment and Shannon stepped quickly out of their way.

The noise of the equipment rolling into the room woke Grant and he stood, moving in beside Shannon.

"You were right," she said, a tear rolling down one side of her face. "He's going to be just fine."

Chapter Thirty

Jimmy spent two weeks in the hospital, gaining strength more each day. His ribs were healing nicely, and the surgery to stop the internal bleeding was successful; he was mending nicely. However, Shannon felt that something deeper inside her brother was broken, and she wasn't sure if that part of him could be repaired.

Once he was awake enough to have non-family visitors, Shannon asked him if he would like to see Raina. After what Raina had said of her last meeting with Jimmy, Shannon didn't want to stress her brother. She was certain he'd been regretting how he'd treated her, but he'd not spoken of her at all.

Jimmy's eyes widened in surprise, then his face fell in shame.

"No. I think it would be better if we just let that go." His hospital bed was raised so he could partially sit up. Jimmy stared at his hands folded across his lap, unable to look his sister in the eye.

"I don't think you're going to want to do that, Jimmy. You need to see her. She has something to tell you."

"Shan, I was so awful to her. I was-" Shannon cut him off mid-sentence.

"-rude, abusive, mean spirited?"

Jimmy shot her a sharp look. "How do you know about Raina, anyway? I never told you about her. And how would you know what our last conversation was like?"

"Yeah, I was wondering why she never came up in any of our conversations," she said with a look of mock dismay. Ignoring his tone, she continued, "We actually found her when we were trying to find you. She told us about the two of you, and yes, she told us what you said to her. I told her you were really going to catch it from me when I found you. But now, well, I just want you to hear her out. She loves you very much."

Jimmy gaped at his sister. "You've got to be kidding. She must hate me and you know it. She'll probably walk in here with a gun and finish the Brevet's job. I can't say I'd blame her. Maybe that wouldn't be such a bad thing."

Raina walked slowly into the room, her eyes filled with tears. "I wouldn't blame me either."

Shannon squeezed Jimmy's hand. "Just hear her out," she said softly, then stepped into the hall where Grant was waiting for her. "They're going to be okay. I can feel that." Shannon's eyes gazed at the doorway to Jimmy's room.

"Oh, you can feel that, can you?" replied Grant with a smirk. "And what makes you such an expert these days?"

Shannon leaned into Grant and kissed him. "*You* make me an expert. You make me better than anything I ever thought I could be."

§§§

Raina moved to the chair beside Jimmy's bed and sat down. The pain on his face was almost more than she could bear.

"I know why you said what you did to me. It was to protect me, but you no longer need to protect me. Am I right?"

"Raina, I-"

"I know, Jimmy. I knew you hated yourself for saying those things the minute the words came out of your mouth. So now, let me tell you what I was *going* to tell you before you so rudely interrupted me that day." Raina smiled softly and took his hand in hers.

Jimmy smiled. "I don't deserve you."

"Well, I'm about to double in bulk here, and you're going to get far more than just me."

The smile faded from Jimmy's face and a look of shock rolled from his eyes to his chin. "You're...You're not...You're..."

"Pregnant. Yes, Jimmy. We're going to be a family, if you'll have us."

Jimmy could hardly breath. Her comment stunned him on so many levels. "If I'll *have* you? *If I'll have you?* I can't believe you would still want me, Raina. I don't know what to say, I'm so happy, and I...I... Yes! Of course I'll have you! And I'll never leave you again, I promise you..."

The joy drained from Jimmy's face as those last words left his lips. The promise he'd just given her made him truly see just how far he'd fallen. He was left with only the bitter taste of his failure as a human being, forced to acknowledge just how much he'd allowed the Brevet organization to take from him.

Raina watched the transformation with alarm. "Jimmy? What is it? What's wrong?"

"I...I don't know if I can keep that promise, Raina. I've done some awful things. I may be going to prison for the rest of my life. I...I may not be able to be there for you and our baby."

Jimmy turned his face away, too ashamed to face the woman who carried his child, the one who'd loved him in spite of himself. The woman he'd tried as hard as he could to erase from his mind, and yet could not. She deserved so much better.

"Jimmy, before either of us jumps to any conclusions, let's see what happens over the next little while, hmm? For right now, I want you to feel the joy of fatherhood. You're going to be a daddy, Jimmy, and I'm going to be a mommy. Let's just live in that thought for right now, because the love that made this new life possible is the one real thing that we know is sure and true. Am I right?"

Jimmy couldn't speak. The words wouldn't come and all he knew, all he could feel in this instant was respect for Raina, for her patience through all he'd done. He never wanted the moment to end. All he could do was squeeze her hand.

Raina understood his wordless response and stood, leaning over his bed and gently hugging him. "I will be there for you, no matter where you are, no matter what you've done. We will get through this together, just like a real family would do, because we *are* a real family."

§§§

There were many meetings and much planning to be done before Jimmy would be truly free of the Brevet organization. Because of his extensive insights and experiences with the organization, Jimmy was generously given the option to turn state's evidence and testify regarding what he knew of the Brevet organization. He gladly accepted the offer. The Brevet group was relatively small for the amount of damage they'd done, but their size made rounding them up easy enough and within a very short time, the organization was incarcerated and awaiting trial.

Investigators from the FBI visited Jimmy regularly after he was released to go home. Until all the Brevet members were in jail, guards were posted at his hospital room and then around his apartment complex when he was released.

Raina stayed at Jimmy's apartment with him through the many interviews and stayed very protective of his recovery, both from the surgery and from the alcohol and drugs. She was unrelenting, especially when she saw him tiring during those interviews. The minute she felt like he'd done all he could do for the day, she sent the investigators packing and ordered Jimmy to bed.

The withdrawal he'd experienced in the warehouse on top of his injuries left him weak and feeling tired much of the time. He slept often, and rested when he wasn't sleeping or in a meeting with the FBI.

On one such day, after a particularly grueling meeting with FBI agents, Raina curled up beside Jimmy on their bed.

"You do this on purpose, you know," he teased her.

"I'm sure I have no idea what you're talking about."

"Right."

Raina snuggled deeper into Jimmy's side. He was partially right. She did love every opportunity she could get to be close to him, even though it never seemed close enough.

"I missed you so much while you were gone, Jimmy. I ached to see you again, even though I wondered if I ever would."

"I wondered that myself. But here we are."

Raina stretched up and kissed Jimmy. "Mostly, I missed getting to do that whenever I wanted."

"You and me both," he said softly. "You and me both."

§§§

"I need to get back to Alaska, you know." Grant and Shannon walked hand in hand through the city park, the sun warm upon their shoulders and getting warmer. Summer was upon them in Iowa. "It is into our busy time for the park. Greyson will need my help."

"I wish you didn't have to go."

The words hung heavy in the air. Never in his life had Grant Mulvane ever been without a response, and he considered his dilemma completely Shannon's doing. He stopped at a park bench and pulled Shannon onto the bench beside him.

"My father always told me it was far easier to speak of difficult things than to hold them inside. I have something I wish to discuss with you."

Shannon turned to face him. "What is it, Grant?"

His eyes met hers and a multitude of emotions tumbled through him, a giant waterfall of the heart. "I told you once that we would speak of us when Jimmy was found. He is found, and we have much to discuss."

Grant took her hands in his and kissed her softly. "I am not complete without you, Shannon, it was not meant that I ever should be. I want us to be together, to be a family our ancestors can be proud of. Shannon, I wish to make what was once a path for one, into a path for two. Our lives will no longer be traveled alone and separate, but will be tied to each other in love. As our time together passes, and if the Spirits are willing, we will make room in our walk through life for children to join us, and we will travel together as a family, now and forever. Will you choose to take this journey with me? Will you marry me?"

The tears that formed in her eyes as Grant spoke, now spilled down her face. She brought his hands to her lips and kissed them softly.

"It would be an honor to walk with you and I promise to make our ancestors proud. Yes, I will marry you, Grant. For now, and for always."

Epilogue

The double ceremony was beautiful, with the couples surrounded by family and friends, in their native land of Alaska. It was a warm summer day when the two new families were made. There was much joy and celebration as the couples were introduced to the attending crowd. Food, dancing, and lots of hugging completed the day.

Jimmy received immunity for his willingness to testify against the Brevet and his testimony not only ended with the incarceration of the members of the organization, it allowed closure for Jimmy. Unsure he would ever be able to forget the awful things he'd done, he was determined to replace the ugliness of his past with the joy that came with having Raina and their child in his life; and as promised, he would never leave them again.

The property where Grant and Shannon's cabin sat was only a small part of the fifteen acres they owned. It was quickly decided that plans for another cabin would be drawn up for Jimmy and Raina. By the time Raina was ready to deliver their son, they'd moved in and set up their home, including a nursery for the new little one.

They named him Clayton James Norton. He would go by Clay, which was also the name of his grandfather. Clay would learn of his native ancestry from his father and his uncle.

There was, however, another reason for the name Clay. Clay comes from the earth, is fashioned into useful utensils and decorative bowls. But it never reaches the full potential of its creation until the formed earth has endured fire, a fire that bakes the raw clay into its designed use, never to be only earth again. Jimmy related very well to this process and had a deep appreciation for it. He only hoped that his son would never have to endure the trial by fire Jimmy had endured.

Grant delighted in introducing Jimmy back into his roots, just as he'd done with Shannon. Raina, Grant and Shannon took great joy, often mixed with times of great anguish, in helping Jimmy slowly heal from his experiences.

The mutual feeling of respect and family between Jimmy and Grant grew quickly. Grant was a never-ending resource as Jimmy worked through the pain of his past.

As for Grant and Shannon…there never was a happier couple. Their love was unique, and grew even deeper as time went by. Two years after their marriage, Shannon gave birth to a stunning little girl, whom they named Abigail, after their mothers. Grant's mother's first name was Abigail and Shannon's mother's middle name was Abigail. They called the little girl Abbie, and she spent many nights on her father's lap, listening to the peaceful calm of his voice telling stories of their native land and their family. But mostly, Grant impressed upon his little girl how very important it was for her to grow up to have integrity, to be true to herself and her ancestors.

It doesn't always happen in life, that we are given a second chance to fix what is broken, unless we work very hard at it. In order for this second chance to make itself known, it is necessary to first discover how the break happened, so that it will never happen again. Jimmy and Grant worked very hard at finding the source of that break in Jimmy, taking long horseback rides together, and talking for hours as they let the peaceful nature of the land rest upon them. The rides, and the talks, helped Jimmy understand what had happened in him, and how to use that knowledge in his recovery.

Shannon had felt that broken, gaping wound in her brother's heart while he was in the hospital. Grant felt it in the warehouse, from his vantage point across the street. The pain was big enough to swallow the whole city. Grant knew he had his work cut out for him then. However, Jimmy was like soft earth, willing to learn, to be taught and grow into something better than he was.

When asked how he created such beautiful statues, Michelangelo once said that it was simply a matter of looking at the piece of marble and then chipping away the parts that didn't belong. So it is with all of us. We are all works in progress.

The End

Other books by JL Redington

Juvenile Series (8-13):

The Esme Chronicles:

A Cry Out of Time
Pirates of Shadowed Time
A View Through Time
A River In Time

Broken Heart Series:

The Lies That Save Us
Solitary Tears
Veiled Secrets
Softly She Leaves
Loves New Dawning

Passions in the Park:

Love Me Anyway
Cherish Me Always
Embrace Me Forever

Duty and Deception:

An Indecent Betrayal
For Love and Liberty

Justice For All:

Lawful Disobedience

Military Privilege
Deadly Recoil

Come join me on
Facebook: Author JL Redington
Email: contact@jlredington.com
Twitter: @jlredington

Made in the USA
Columbia, SC
17 May 2017